LOVE BEC

"Don't you believe in magic?" Harlequin asked. "You should, because you weave spells of your own. You hold me in thrall at this very moment, and while your magic surrounds me, I am safe from the worst that the world can do."

"But can't you tell me – ?"

Swiftly his hand was across her mouth.

"No," he said seriously. "I can tell you nothing, except that you must believe in me. Is that so hard?"

"Not when you are here with me. But you will go again, and then I may be afraid, and lose faith."

"No, you will not," he said at once. "Because you are brave, and you know that I will never really leave you. And one day – "

"One day ?" Rona whispered eagerly.

"One day, God willing, our time will come. In the mean time – "

He gathered her in his arms and pressed his lips to hers.

THE BARBARA CARTLAND PINK COLLECTION

Titles in this series

LOVE BECAME THEIRS

BARBARA CARTLAND

Barbaracartland.com Ltd

THE BARBARA CARTLAND PINK COLLECTION

Dame Barbara Cartland is still regarded as the most prolific bestselling author in the history of the world.

In her lifetime she was frequently in the Guinness Book of Records for writing more books than any other living author.

Her most amazing literary feat was to double her output from 10 books a year to over 20 books a year when she was 77 to meet the huge demand.

She went on writing continuously at this rate for 20 years and wrote her very last book at the age of 97, thus completing an incredible 400 books between the ages of 77 and 97.

Her publishers finally could not keep up with this phenomenal output, so at her death in 2000 she left behind an amazing 160 unpublished manuscripts, something that no other author has ever achieved.

Barbara's son, Ian McCorquodale, together with his daughter Iona, felt that it was their sacred duty to publish all these titles for Barbara's millions of admirers all over the world who so love her wonderful romances.

So in 2004 they started publishing the 160 brand new Barbara Cartlands as *The Barbara Cartland Pink Collection*, as Barbara's favourite colour was always pink – and yet more pink!

The Barbara Cartland Pink Collection is published monthly exclusively by Barbaracartland.com and the books are numbered in sequence from 1 to 160.

Enjoy receiving a brand new Barbara Cartland book each month by taking out an annual subscription to the Pink Collection, or purchase the books individually.

The Pink Collection is available from the Barbara Cartland website www.barbaracartland.com, via mail order and through all good bookshops.

In addition Ian and Iona are proud to announce that The Barbara Cartland Pink Collection is now available in ebook format as from Valentine's Day 2011.

For more information, please contact us at:

Barbaracartland.com Ltd.
Camfield Place
Hatfield
Hertfordshire AL9 6JE
United Kingdom

Telephone: +44 (0)1707 642629
Fax: +44 (0)1707 663041
Email: info@barbaracartland.com

THE LATE DAME BARBARA CARTLAND

Barbara Cartland who sadly died in May 2000 at the age of nearly 99 was the world's most famous romantic novelist who wrote 723 books in her lifetime with worldwide sales of over 1 billion copies and her books were translated into 36 different languages.

As well as romantic novels, she wrote historical biographies, 6 autobiographies, theatrical plays, books of advice on life, love, vitamins and cookery. She also found time to be a political speaker and television and radio personality

She wrote her first book at the age of 21 and this was called Jigsaw. It became an immediate bestseller and sold 100,000 copies in hardback and was translated into 6 different languages. She wrote continuously throughout her life, writing bestsellers for an astonishing 76 years. Her books have always been immensely popular in the United States, where in 1976 her current books were at numbers 1 & 2 in the B. Dalton bestsellers list, a feat never achieved before or since by any author.

Barbara Cartland became a legend in her own lifetime and will be best remembered for her wonderful romantic novels, so loved by her millions of readers throughout the world.

Her books will always be treasured for their moral message, her pure and innocent heroines, her good looking and dashing heroes and above all her belief that the power of love is more important than anything else in everyone's life.

"Love can change in time, but true love never changes."

Barbara Cartland

CHAPTER ONE
1867

A masked ball! And in fancy dress.

What could be more wonderful?

Rona Trafford was humming to herself as she turned this way and that before the mirror, revelling in the beauty of her dress.

It was made of gleaming white satin brocade, in the eighteenth century style, with wide panniers at the sides, and a tight bodice. She knew it enhanced her beauty, showing her dainty figure and tiny waist to advantage. She would make a sensation and, at nineteen, she was young enough to enjoy that.

Her mother bustled in. She was dressed as Queen Elizabeth and looked very imperious, but her face lit up with a most unroyal glee when she saw her daughter.

"There'll be nobody to touch you, my darling!" she exclaimed. "What jewels are you going to wear?"

"I thought the pearls, Mama," said Rona, holding up a pearl necklace.

"Hmm! Very nice," said Mrs. Trafford doubtfully. "But I think diamonds would be better."

She opened the black box that she was carrying, revealing a heavy diamond necklace. It had three strands of completely perfect jewels, and had obviously cost a king's ransom. There were matching ear rings and bracelet.

Rona gasped.

"Mama! How can I possibly wear those? They're yours."

"But I want to see them on you, my dear. You'll look so lovely in them."

"But Lady Harris says an unmarried girl should avoid diamonds or, if she must wear them, no more than a discreet pendant."

Lady Harris' word was usually considered law in the Trafford household. She was the wife of a Knight, and made much of her knowledge of society, which impressed Rona's parents, who had no title at all to boast of. But tonight Rona's mother rebelled.

"I don't think we should take Lady Harris' opinions too seriously, my love. I know for a fact that she has not been invited to the Duchess of Westminster's ball tonight. We, on the other hand, have been invited. Royalty will be present. It is an occasion for showing ourselves at our best."

"At our wealthiest, you mean," replied Rona impishly.

"My dear, I beg of you not to say things like that. It is thoroughly vulgar."

"But that's what Lady Harris says, that an heiress who puffs off her wealth is vulgar."

"I don't want to hear another word about Lady Harris," said Mrs. Trafford firmly. "She will not be at Westminster House tonight."

"But would we be going to Westminster House if it wasn't known that Papa was terribly rich?" asked Rona.

Her mother gave a little scream.

"A young girl shouldn't concern herself with such matters," she said. "Now, not another word. You will wear the diamonds, and you will outshine any other woman there."

"Yes, Mama," Rona said, with apparent meekness.

"Well, you always do outshine the others," said Mrs. Trafford cheerfully. "You've been the belle of the season. Just think. Westminster House!"

"I'm really looking forward to seeing it. They say it has the most magnificent pictures."

"You'll be too busy dancing to notice the pictures. And who knows what may happen tonight?"

"Why should anything special happen tonight?"

Mrs. Trafford put her finger over her lips.

"Let's just say that a certain young man is very interested in you."

That made Rona frown a little. Casting her mind back over the young men she had met in her glittering season, she could not recall a single one who had greatly interested her. She thought that the pictures she had read about would certainly be more interesting than the average young man.

Older men seemed more intelligent, and certainly had a wider range of knowledge.

"Aren't you going to ask me who is it?" her Mama quizzed her archly. "Well, I'm sure you can guess. He's been so particular in his attentions, and I've noticed how much you enjoyed them."

Since Rona could not think of any man who had been particular in his attentions, still less one who had inspired her to enjoyment, she was left wondering.

When the diamonds were draped about her neck it was time for the wig to be fitted on. It was shining silver white, dressed high on her head, with two ringlets falling down onto her left shoulder, and it revealed her beautiful, long, slender neck, which one admirer had likened to that of a swan.

Finally, the mask. It was white satin, fringed with lace, decorated with silver spangles.

"You look mysterious and enchanting," Mama assured her.

Rona picked up an elegant fan which matched the mask, and gave her mother a deep curtsy, smiling with pleasurable anticipation of the evening ahead. Laughing, Mama returned the curtsy, and they left the room together to go down the great stairway to find Papa.

But there was no sign of him in the hall and the butler explained that Mr. Trafford had been delayed and would be down in a moment.

"Yes, and I know what has delayed him," Mama murmured to her daughter. "Primping in front of the mirror. I vow, men are worse than we are. Wait in the library, darling. I must speak to cook to make sure she knows what refreshments your Papa wants left out tonight. The last time, she left sandwiches instead of cake and he was so cross."

She bustled away. Rona went into the library and sat down on a wide leather sofa, careful not to crease her lovely dress. This morning's copy of *The Times* lay on a low table, and to pass the time she began to browse through it.

There was a report of a debate in the House of Lords which she tried to find interesting, and failed. They all seemed to say the same thing, at great length.

Idly turning the pages, she came to an advertisement from an agency, and perused it, almost without realising she was doing so.

After an advertisement for a secretary, a cook and several demands for coachmen who were well-trained, she read,

'Wanted for a girl of sixteen, English governess who is prepared to travel abroad. Must be able to teach French, German and most European languages.'

'I expect they'll have difficulty finding an English

governess who is good at languages,' she thought. 'Mama always thought my governesses were hopeless at teaching me French.'

She remembered how finally her father and mother had taken her to Paris where they stayed with friends. She had managed, by the time they left, to speak French almost fluently. And she had enjoyed Paris.

'So lovely,' she mused happily now. 'And all those gorgeous clothes.'

The following year when her father had taken her to stay with one of his friends who lived in Germany, she was able, by the time they left, to speak and understand ordinary German. Her father's friends had said they had never known an English girl who had mastered their language so quickly.

In fact they had praised her intelligence so much that Mama had hushed them, somewhat embarrassed. Girls weren't supposed to be brainy, and a reputation for cleverness might harm Rona's marriage prospects.

At last she heard Papa's voice in the hall and hurried out. He exclaimed with pleasure at the sight of her, and paid a compliment to Mama, who had also hurried back, so as not to keep them waiting.

He was in a genial mood tonight, Rona was glad to see. Papa had an uncertain temper, which became unpleasant when he was thwarted. He spoiled and indulged his wife and daughter, showering costly gifts on them. But he expected to be obeyed.

In fact, he reminded Rona of Henry VIII, the bullying Tudor king who had also smiled when he got his own way, and turned nasty when he did not. When he had been choosing his costume, Rona had suggested Henry VIII to him, half fearful, lest he should suspect her of satire. But he had embraced the suggestion eagerly, and seemed unaware that it might have a personal application.

"What splendid ladies," he said now. "I shall be the envy of every man there."

They, in turn, complimented him on his magnificent appearance, and the atmosphere was very jolly.

As the maid was settling the cloak about her shoulders, Rona became aware that her parents were whispering.

"Have you told her?" she just heard her father ask.

"Just a hint," replied her mother. "I'm sure she understands everything."

'But I don't understand anything,' thought Rona. 'What's going to happen that I'm supposed to know all about? Who is it that has been 'particular in his attentions', and if I've enjoyed them so much that Mama has noticed, why haven't I noticed?'

It was strange to be moving towards such a mystery, but she soon forgot that in the pleasure of the ball. It was high summer and they travelled to Westminster House in an open carriage. Normally Mr. Trafford enjoyed the stares of onlookers, interpreting this as admiration of the family's wealth. But tonight he was less at ease.

"They're daring to laugh at us," he muttered.

"Well, you can't blame them, Papa," chuckled Rona. "It's not every day that they see Henry VIII and Queen Elizabeth riding together."

He scowled, and now he thought of something else that displeased him.

"Did you have to wear that wig?" he asked. It completely covers your hair."

"It's eighteenth century, Papa. In those days they wore wigs, men too."

"But your own hair's so pretty." His grudging voice robbed the words of generosity.

Luckily they were soon at Westminster House, where

a stream of other carriages, also bearing colourful characters, were also arriving.

As soon as they entered the great house, they heard the sound of music coming from the ballroom at the back of the house. Crowds of strangely dressed guests were streaming along the broad hall to where the Duke and Duchess stood in the doorway waiting to greet their guests. They exclaimed in delight at the Trafford family, and Rona saw the Duchess cast a knowing eye over her diamonds.

Then they were inside the ballroom. At first Rona felt almost giddy from the bright lights and the whirling couples. There was Cleopatra, dancing with a Sultan in gold robes, and Anne Boleyn dancing with a bear, while King Charles I shared a glass of champagne with a parrot. It all looked like enormous fun.

"Ah, look who I see," said her father, suddenly genial again.

Rona followed his gaze to Lord Robert Horton. He was a handsome man whose looks, Rona had always thought, were spoiled by a permanently superior expression. He was dressed as a Regency dandy, with a high neck cloth, knee breeches and swallow tailed coat. There was no doubt that it suited his elegant figure.

Lord Robert's estate ran beside the Trafford estate, and he had several times stayed with them at The Court, their country house. He rode to hounds with her father and flirted with any married women who happened to be in their party, but it was rare for him to speak to Rona, whom he had seemed to consider unworthy of his lofty attention.

Lord Robert had seen them and was making his way towards them. Over his face he wore a black silk mask, which he removed as he approached.

"Sir, ladies." He made a neat bow. "A pleasure to see you. Miss Trafford, may I beg the first dance?"

Rona was about to make an excuse, for Lord Robert had never been a favourite of hers, but her father hurried to speak first.

"Certainly you may. You make a delightful couple and I think you will both be an example of good dancing to the rest of the party."

Lord Robert laughed.

"That's a compliment I don't usually receive from you," he replied, "especially when we're in the hunting field."

"You are now in a field of beautiful women," Mr. Trafford said. "If you ask me, although I am prejudiced, I think my daughter wins the race."

"Of course she does," Lord Robert agreed. "That's why I am determined to open the ball with her and she is undoubtedly too pretty to be anything but the belle of the evening."

He spoke so fervently that Rona was astonished. Since when had he thought her so pretty? During his last visit to The Court, her parents had given a ball and he had not even danced with her, although, as the daughter of his hosts, she was entitled to that courtesy.

She would have liked to refuse him this dance but she was now in an impossible position. Neither did Lord Robert wait for her answer, apparently thinking that her father's consent made it unnecessary.

Before she knew where she was he had replaced his mask, put his arms round her and drawn her on to the floor. He danced very well, and at first she had to concentrate on equalling him.

As she grew more confident, she had time to look around and she became aware that she was being watched.

A man dressed in a Harlequin costume, was standing by the French windows, his eyes fixed on the dancers – no, on *her*, she realised. As she was swept around by the dance she lost sight of him, but then another turn would bring him back into view.

And he was always looking at her.

It was as though nobody else existed in the room.

He was a tall man, with a lean figure that was admirably displayed by the close fitting, diamond patterned costume. On his head was a black tricorne hat, around his neck was a small white ruff, and his face was largely concealed by a black mask.

It was strange, she thought, that she should be so certain that he was watching her, when she only glimpsed him now and then, and he was too far away for her to see his eyes properly. All she could discern through the slits in his mask was a gleam, and yet she knew, beyond a shadow of doubt, that the gleam was for her.

It was as though the Harlequin was speaking to her in a strange, silent language that only they could understand. There was something slightly sinister about him as he stood there, very still, almost as if he were warning her of something.

"Miss Trafford!" Lord Robert was addressing her with a slight edge on his voice.

"I'm sorry," she said hastily. "What did you say?"

"I complimented you on your appearance, but you made no answer."

"I beg your pardon. I was absorbed in admiring – admiring everything around us," she finished. It was the best she could manage.

"You must be very absorbed not to hear me say that you are the most beautiful girl here tonight."

"Why, how can you know how I look when my mask conceals so much of my face?" she asked trying to sound light-hearted.

"But I have seen your face before," he reminded her, "so naturally I know that you are beautiful, despite your mask."

Rona tried to look flattered, but this plodding attempt at gallantry set her teeth on edge. There was something about the heaviness of Lord Robert's mind that reminded her of a suet pudding.

She murmured, "too kind," and turned her head as the French windows came into view again.

But the Harlequin had gone.

She forced herself to pay attention to Lord Robert's ponderous conversation. It was as though he had read a book on 'How to make light conversation at a ball.' He was following the instructions dutifully, but it was hard going for them both.

"This party is brilliant," he said. "It's just like the ones your father and mother give. They always manage to make everyone they entertain feel they are stepping into fairyland."

"Do you really think that?" Rona asked. "I thought when you were last staying with us in the country, you found it rather dull."

"Not at all. I enjoyed every moment of it, especially riding your father's horses. They are some of the best I've ever encountered."

"I hope you said that to Papa," Rona replied trying to sound amiable. "He loves being complimented on his stable."

"Your father and I understand each other pretty well," said Lord Robert.

She frowned. The words might have been meant pleasantly, yet somehow they grated on her.

To her relief the music was ending. She tried to

disengage herself, but he kept his arm around her waist.

"I hope you will grant me the next dance as well," he said.

"You are too kind, but I don't think I should do so," she said, trying to sound firm.

"Your father will not object."

"But I will object," she said, becoming annoyed.

His brow darkened. "You object to dancing with me?"

"I object to being taken for granted. Will you please release me?"

He hesitated and she was sure he was on the verge of refusing when a voice startled them both.

"There you are! I've been looking for you."

The Harlequin had appeared, as if through a trapdoor. He danced right round the two of them before seizing Rona's hand.

"You promised me the next dance," he said. "Don't say you've forgotten."

Lord Robert's lips tightened.

"It's quite impossible that Miss Trafford – "

"No, that's too bad of you," Harlequin rushed on, ignoring him. "Come along, you're not getting out of it now."

Before she could catch her breath, he pulled her free from Lord Robert's restraining arm and swept her away. The music struck up again and they were whirling, whirling around the floor in a dizzying waltz.

"You shouldn't have done that," Rona said when she could catch your breath.

"Why not?"

"He knew I hadn't promised you a dance."

"Nonsense, you promised me at our last meeting."

"Did – did I?"

"I find it very sad that you should have forgotten," he said, sounding hurt.

"But we've never met before. You're playing tricks."

"Of course. That's what a Harlequin does. He's a master of tricks. He can dazzle with deception, and read people's minds. That's how he knows when a damsel is in distress, and needs him to come to her rescue."

"I don't know what you – " she began to say primly.

Then she stopped. This mysterious man really did seem able to read the thoughts she was trying to conceal, so perhaps it was useless to try to deceive him.

"Was it that obvious?" she asked with something close to despair.

"I saw you enter the ballroom. I saw him advance on you like a predator pouncing on a lamb, a tethered lamb, since you were given no chance to refuse. Henry VIII was very determined to make you accept, wasn't he?"

"Yes, I'm afraid he was. He's my father. I suppose he thought it would be rude for me to refuse."

"Or maybe he's trying to marry you to the fellow."

"Oh no," she said quickly. "He knows that I have no particular liking for Lord Robert – "

"I wonder if he does know. He doesn't look to me like the kind of man who interests himself in other people's feelings if they run contrary to his own."

This gave Rona an uneasy feeling. It was so completely true of Papa.

Harlequin could read people's secrets. But surely he could not be right about her father wanting her to marry Lord Robert? She tried to silence the memory of certain signs and remarks that had made her uneasy that evening.

"Was that why you were watching me?" she asked.

"Because you thought I was a damsel in distress?"

"Yes, I wanted to see if my first impression of you had been correct. Your initial reluctance might not have meant very much. You could have been madly in love with him, but had a violent quarrel."

"I can't imagine any woman being madly in love with *him*," she said frankly.

"Nor I. And when I saw you dancing together, I knew that wasn't the explanation. You held yourself stiffly, and kept your distance. People don't dance like that when they're in love."

"Indeed?" she said, slightly offended. This fellow was growing impertinent. "You think you know all about it?"

"Harlequin knows all about everything," he said outrageously.

"Then I think you must be quite insufferable," she said, trying not to laugh.

"I am," he said at once. "Completely insufferable. Most people want to kick me after quite a short acquaintance."

This time she did laugh. It was impossible to stay annoyed with this joker.

"That's better," he said. "You have such a pretty mouth. It ought to laugh often. It's a shame that I can't see more of your face, but your mouth will do – for a while, at any rate."

"You are shameless, sir," she said, trying to sound severe.

"Totally shameless," he agreed promptly.

"If we were not wearing masks, I could never listen to you talking like this."

"You're right. One can say almost anything from behind a mask. I can say, for instance, that among the many subjects on which Harlequin is an expert, is love. You don't love that man, and he doesn't love you. Don't let them make you marry him."

"There's no question of my marrying him. Nobody but you has even thought of it."

"I only wish you were right, but you are not. I simply want to put you on your guard."

"That's very kind of you, and although I disagree, I am grateful to you for rescuing me. Now, please tell me who you are. Without knowing your name I shouldn't even be talking to you, much less dancing with you."

He was silent.

"Sir, I insist that you tell me your name."

"My name is Harlequin, and I am a lover of fair ladies. I sigh at their feet, I kiss the hems of their garments as they float past. I watch and protect them, and rescue them from danger."

"I never heard of Harlequin as a lover of ladies," Rona replied, briefly abandoning the attempt to make him serious. "He's a joker and a trickster, who has to be rescued when he himself gets into a muddle."

"They lie who say it!" he declared theatrically. "Slanders, ma'am. Believe none of it."

She chuckled. He might not be quite proper, but he was exceedingly diverting.

"I also heard," she teased him, "that if it weren't for Columbine he'd be in even more trouble."

"Good heavens!" he cried. "Unmasked. My secrets are all revealed. It's true, I cannot deny it. Each man needs his Columbine to keep him on the straight and narrow. Are you Columbine? You look like it, all in white."

"Indeed no," she said firmly. "I'm an eighteenth century lady." She was falling in with his mood, finding it surprisingly easy to talk back to him in his own style. Not knowing who he was seemed to matter less as he whirled her about.

"Of course you are," he said. "A lady of the court. You have danced with kings and princes."

"And I also think," she could not resist adding, "that it would take more than my efforts to keep you on the straight and narrow."

He roared with laughter, showing strong white teeth. He was holding her improperly close but, strangely, she had no desire to back away from him, such as she had felt with Lord Robert. Instead, she found herself looking at his mouth, which was very near.

It was a wide, mobile mouth, that looked as though it was made for laughing, and it made her wonder about the rest of his face. He was certainly a young man. She could tell that from the strength of the hands clasping her, and his lithe, graceful movements with their unmistakeable hint of power.

He was very tall. Rona was tall herself, but he towered over her by a good eight inches. Beyond that, all she knew was his mouth. The face above was concealed by the black mask, with only the eyes showing through the slits. She could just see that they were blue, the most intense blue that she had ever seen. They gleamed with life and wit, and something that might even have been danger. She could not be sure.

The music was coming to an end. As the dance slowed Rona could see Lord Robert approaching, with a look on his face that said he would not be denied.

"Oh dear," she sighed.

"Remember," Harlequin murmured, "Don't let yourself be forced into anything."

Lord Robert presented himself in her path, holding out

his hand for her.

"You will not be so cruel as to refuse to dance with me," he said. It was an assertion, not a question.

In fact his whole manner was of a man determined to have his own way, and for a moment Rona wondered whether Harlequin's suspicions might be correct.

But surely that was absurd.

Nobody could force her into anything she did not want to do.

Just the same, as Lord Robert led her away, she took a final look over her shoulder to where Harlequin stood watching.

Then he melted into the crowd, leaving her feeling rather lonely.

CHAPTER TWO

Rona had expected Lord Robert to lead her into the dance, but instead he continued walking out of the ballroom into the garden, hung with fairy lights.

"You asked me to dance," she protested.

"I have something to say to you," he replied, not slowing.

This high handed behaviour was not at all to her taste, but she followed him, thinking that at any moment he would stop, but he kept on walking. When he finally indicated for her to sit on one of the rustic benches, they were well away from the lights.

"It's very dark," Rona said, sitting reluctantly.

"That's why I've brought you here," Robert replied. "What I have to say to you I do not want overheard."

Her heart beat with apprehension. If only there was some way to stop him! But there was no way, so she resigned herself to listening.

He cleared his throat, sounding uncomfortable.

"It is quite simple," he said abruptly. "I love you, and I want you to marry me."

She had been half expecting it, yet now she found herself breathless and miserable. She did not want to marry this man. She wanted only to get away from him.

"You surprise me," she managed to say, "because I hardly know you."

"That is ridiculous," he replied, with a brusqueness that sat oddly with the proposal he was making. "I've stayed several times at your house in the country, and we got to know each other then."

"No, we didn't," she said rebelliously. "You scarcely spoke to me."

"I have always thought how beautiful you were," he pressed on determinedly. "But I suppose I was too shy to ask you then to be my wife."

"Shy?" she exclaimed. "You?"

That might not be polite, but she could not help herself. He was talking nonsense, and it occurred to her that he had learned his speech by heart and could not cope with unscripted interruptions.

He ignored her words and fell silent, looking into her face, as though expecting an appropriate response. When she did not speak he went on,

"Now things are different. You are grown-up, you have 'come out'. You may be a debutante but you are definitely old enough for men to love you and to want you to belong to them."

He waited again, but she remained stubbornly silent, hoping to discourage him.

It was a forlorn hope.

"Before anyone else snatches you up," he ground on determinedly, "I want you to listen to me when I say I love you, and I want you as my wife."

As he spoke he moved a little nearer and put his arm round her shoulders.

"I love you," he recited again. "You are so beautiful that I am terrified someone will take you away from me."

He did not sound terrified, or in love. He sounded like a man relieved to have got to the end of his prepared speech without forgetting it.

Suddenly he pulled her towards him and managed to press his lips on hers before she could stop him.

For a moment Rona held still, trying to decide how she felt about this. Did Lord Robert's kiss transport her to the stars, fill her with joy, make her heart beat faster with rapture?

No.

She turned her head sharply away but he didn't release her. Instead he attempted to put his arms further around her, trying to kiss her again. His lips brushed her cheek and he tried to pull her head towards him, which she firmly resisted.

"Tell me that you will love me and be my wife!" he grated.

"I cannot – do – that," she replied, "because – I hardly – know you and I have – not thought – about you in – that way."

She stammered a little over the words, and Lord Robert said,

"You have to think of me, I will make you think of me. I will make you want me, and I know that once we are married we will be very, very happy."

He would have pulled her closer and kissed her again but Rona deftly managed to loosen his grasp, saying as she did so,

"I'll think about it. I will let you know, but I must have time to think."

"Why need you think about something that is so obvious?" he said with a touch of impatience.

She was growing very annoyed.

"It is not obvious to me," she said.

"That's because you're not looking at it in the right way," he said. "If you consider the matter properly our marriage makes sense."

She stared at him, wondering if he really thought this was how a man proposed.

"It is in every way suitable," he continued. "Your father has given his blessing – "

"What?" Angrily Rona rose to her feet. "You spoke to my father before me?"

"Certainly. I could not have married you without his consent."

"You cannot marry me without *my* consent," she said. "I think we have said enough. I will consider your most flattering offer – " She spoke ironically, but she doubted he was astute enough to realise it, "and let you know my decision. Now I am going back to the house."

"I think you should remain, and hear me out," he said firmly. "Perhaps I have not expressed myself well. I have told you that I love you, but I should have spoken longer about the – ah – depth of my passion. For some time now you have filled my thoughts and dreams – "

"Please," she said hastily. "I assure you it is needless for you to say more. We will talk later."

He reached out to restrain her, but she dodged away and began to run in the direction of the house. She was in turmoil, not only at the proposal, but at the discovery that Lord Robert had virtually settled the matter with her father first.

'Almost as though it did not concern me at all,' she thought angrily.

And again she remembered Harlequin's warnings.

She tried to slip into the house unobtrusively and mingle with the crowd. But then she saw her parents, and realised that they were looking for her, eager to know what had happened.

"Alone, my dear?" asked her father, too jovially. "Surely I saw you come in from the garden? I hope you weren't wandering there unchaperoned?"

"I was with Lord Robert. You must forgive me, Papa. I realise that it was improper of me to go out there with him alone."

She said this because she was curious to know how he would react, after what she had just heard.

"My dear, I'm sure it can be overlooked in the circumstances."

"What circumstances, Papa?"

"Well, you and Lord Robert – I'm sure he behaved like a gentleman – but if his ardour carried him away – well, heh, heh!"

"Lord Robert proposed marriage."

"Did he? Did he indeed? Well, well!"

"And I told him I would consider the matter. Then I returned to the house."

"Very proper, my dear. But now you have spoken to me it will be quite correct for you to show your affection for him."

"But I have no affection for him, Papa."

"Nonsense, nonsense! Of course you have," he responded sharply.

"No Papa, he doesn't please me at all."

"What foolishness is this? You don't know what you feel. Take my word for it, you'll be very happy."

"But I – "

"Ah, there he is! Lord Robert, my child has been speaking to me – "

"Papa – "

But her father ignored her distress, seized her hand, then seized Lord Robert's hand, and forced their two hands together.

"What a fine couple you will make!" he exclaimed. "How proud I am!"

Lord Robert inclined his head towards Rona.

"Miss Trafford, I take it this means you accept my proposal."

"No sir," said Rona, summoning all her courage. "I have not yet made a decision. My father was being premature. Excuse me!"

She heard her father's sharp intake of breath at this defiance, and knew that he would be very angry with her later. But just now she had to get away. Snatching her hand free she turned and fled.

She soon realised that she was not to be allowed to escape so easily, but at least it was Mama who came running after her.

"My dear child, don't be so hasty! Stop a moment. I'm out of breath."

Rona relented and turned to face her mother, who was puffing in a way that violently agitated her ruff.

"I won't be forced, Mama."

"Who says anything about forcing? Don't be silly."

"Both Papa and Lord Robert would force me if they could. Oh, he was right! Why didn't I see it?"

"He? Who?"

"Nobody," she said hastily. She could not tell Mama about Harlequin and his predictions. He seemed even more mysterious now that she knew he had seen and understood so much.

"Lord Robert is infatuated with you, darling," her mother said. "In fact he told me you were the most beautiful, the most charming and the most entrancing girl he had ever met."

"Yes, he told me I was beautiful," Rona said. "But

he's never spoken like that before."

"Perhaps you didn't give him the chance. A man is shy of telling you he loves you the first time."

Shy. There was that word again. Anyone less shy than Lord Robert it would be hard to imagine. She began to wonder if her Mama had actually coached him.

"You must encourage him," Mrs. Trafford continued.

"The truth is, Mama, I don't find him at all attractive," Rona said.

Her mother stared at her.

"But why? After all he is very good-looking and he has a title."

"Not much of a title. He isn't an Earl or a Viscount, or anything like that."

"But his father is the Duke of Cannington. It's true that he won't be a Duke himself, as he has three older brothers, who aren't likely to die unfortunately, except for one who's in the army."

"Mama!" said Rona, scandalised.

"Well, we must be realistic."

"I am being realistic. I see nothing in him to like."

"But you would be part of a Ducal family, and invited to Cannington Towers every Christmas. They say royalty sometimes goes there."

"Mama, when I marry I want it to be a man that I love. I really don't care where we go for Christmas."

"Love is something which comes unexpectedly, but inevitably," Mama said. "And, darling, I want you to marry someone who will love you, take care of you and as your father said, young men with titles are few and far between."

"Then I'll marry a man without a title."

"Oh don't say that," said Mama with a little gasp.

"Papa would be so angry. He's set his heart on this marriage."

"What about my heart, Mama? Doesn't that count at all?"

"But my dear child, love follows marriage for a respectable girl. Of course you will love your husband. That is a wife's duty. Now, be a good girl, and come back with me."

She had a feeling that a net was tightening around her. If she went back now she would be lost.

"No, Mama. I cannot return with you. I have promised a dance to – to – "

"To me," said Harlequin from the shadows. He bowed to Mrs. Trafford. "Your servant ma'am."

Before either of the ladies could reply he had seized Rona's hand and drawn her well away.

"Thank goodness you were there," she said. "But how?"

"Harlequin is everywhere, and sees everything. I knew you would be needing me."

"Oh, you were right," she said bitterly. "You were right about everything. How could I be so blind?"

"We are all blind when we are betrayed by those we trust," he said, and for once he was not laughing. "You trusted your parents so you never thought they would pressure you like this. But now you'll be on your guard."

He paused to take two glasses of champagne from a footman, and continued walking beside her until they were well away from the house and were walking deep into the garden, through the fairy lights, and beyond, into the darkness.

It was strange, she thought, that it did not trouble her to come here with this stranger, when she had been so

24

reluctant with Lord Robert. She felt safe with Harlequin, even though he called himself a trickster.

He found a garden seat. They sat down together and he handed her a glass of champagne.

"So he declared himself?" he said. "I saw your father put your hands together."

"I haven't accepted him but Papa is determined to make me. He's so set on the idea that I can't make him understand that I don't want to."

"Why does he want it so much?"

"He hates the idea of me inheriting his estate unless I have a husband to run it. He says no woman has enough brains to run anything.

"Lord Robert's own land runs beside ours, so of course that makes him suitable to Papa. And the other thing – well – Lord Robert's father is a Duke, which Papa thinks is wonderful."

"But you don't?"

"I don't see that it matters. I wouldn't marry a man just because he had a title, but only if we loved each other more than anything else in the world."

"Ah yes, that's what we all want," said Harlequin reflectively. "But it can be hard to find. And when you have found the right person, how can you be really sure?"

"You can be quite certain when you've found the wrong person," Rona said firmly. "I told Lord Robert that I would think over his proposal, but I was playing for time. I knew he was the wrong person as soon as he kissed me."

"You let him kiss you?"

"No, I didn't let him, I couldn't stop him. I hated it. It was like kissing a haddock."

"I bow to your superior knowledge of haddock, ma'am," he said gravely.

She chuckled, and felt a little better.

"How did you know it was all going to happen?" she asked him.

"The world is a wicked place."

Something in his voice made her say,

"You spoke of being blind when we are betrayed by those we trust. You know about that, don't you?"

He shrugged. "Perhaps. Perhaps not."

"No." She laid a hand on his arm. "Don't tease me now. I'm serious."

"I'm sorry" Harlequin replied. Yes, I know how easily you can blind yourself with trust, and how cruel betrayal can be."

"Won't you tell me about it? You know so much about me, it isn't fair that I know nothing about you."

He was silent and she peered at him, trying to see some of his face. But the mask hid most of it, and the darkness hid the rest.

Yet she could sense his tension, as though he were struggling with a great decision. There was something burdening him, something he needed to speak of, and in another moment he would tell her.

The she heard the sound of voices from somewhere behind them.

The spell was broken. He would not tell her now. She thought she heard him give a sigh, but she could not be sure.

"It's better if we let things be," he said at last.

"I suppose we should return," she said reluctantly. "No, wait!" she added sharply. For she had recognised one of the voices.

"What is it?" asked Harlequin.

"Lord Robert. He mustn't find me here."

"Then let us keep quite still and silent, and the darkness will hide us," Harlequin whispered.

They sat there, hardly breathing. Suddenly Lord Robert's voice came again, louder.

"What the devil are you doing here?"

Then a girl's voice. "Oh Robert, darling, please don't be angry with me. I had to come."

There was the sound of skirts rustling, as though she were running to him.

"Oh darling, darling," she cried passionately. "I couldn't bear it a moment longer. Kiss me. Kiss me."

"Doreen, for pity's sake!" he exclaimed.

Rona sat up sharply.

"Doreen!" she said. "I know her. She lives near me in the country. I thought her voice was familiar. I didn't know that she was in London."

Doreen was speaking again,

"They say you're going to marry – "

"Hush!" Robert said violently. "Don't speak of that. It's none of your business who I marry."

There was a cry and a sob.

"None of my business? How can you be so cruel? You said you would marry me."

"I said I would like to if I could afford it," he replied harshly. "I never proposed to you."

"But you did say you loved me."

"Yes, and I do love you. I would far rather marry you than that boring girl I asked tonight. But I can't. My estate is falling to pieces and I need money. She has it, or rather her father has. He'll pay me anything I ask, just to connect his family with a Duke."

He broke off and there was only the sound of her sobbing.

Rona could not move. The whole world seemed to have contracted down to this spot, the sound of the two voices, one anguished, one callous.

She was trembling with shock, and barely conscious of the fact that Harlequin had taken her hand between two of his own, and was holding it comfortingly.

Lord Robert's voice came again, a little kinder, but still irritated.

"Stop crying, there's a good girl. I do love you, but it can't be helped. Now come along, stop that."

Again there was a rustling sound, as if he had taken hold of her. Then silence.

Rona set her chin as she rose from the bench and began to walk in the direction of the couple.

"Better not look," murmured Harlequin, in step beside her. "It'll only upset you more."

"I'm not upset," she murmured back. "I'm furious."

She found a gap between the trees and through it she could see, illuminated by moonlight, the sight of Lord Robert and Doreen passionately embracing. She stood frozen, watching them, until Lord Robert drew back.

"Not here," he said. "Someone may see us. Come."

He took Doreen's hand and drew her away into the darkness, leaving the other two standing there.

It was a long time before Rona could force herself to move. Her mind was in a turmoil of misery.

She was not in love with Lord Robert, and for that she must be thankful. She pitied the unfortunate Doreen, betrayed by a selfish man who put money above the love that might have been his.

But although she did not have a broken heart, her feelings were bitter and wretched. Only a few hours ago the world had been a delightful place, where there was music and beautiful clothes, and endless pleasure.

Now it had suddenly become monstrous, a place of treachery, greed and lies.

"How could he?" she exclaimed angrily. "How could he treat that poor girl like that, when she loves him, and he says he loves her?"

"But he told her why," said Harlequin. "He needs your money."

"Oh yes! You should have heard what he said to me earlier tonight – pretending to love me, saying he wanted to marry me. And all the time he was being selfish and deceitful."

"But at least you know the truth now."

"About him, yes, but what about the others? How true are their hearts? All the men who want to dance with me at balls, and flirt with me. I always knew that Papa's fortune was a lure, but only in the back of my mind. But this is what it really means. Lies and treachery and greed. Now I think all men must be the same."

"No," Harlequin said quickly. "Men are not all the same. Some are honest and faithful. You must trust to heaven that one day you will meet the man you spoke about – the one who will love you more than anything else in the world. He's out there, somewhere in the world, looking for you."

"No, no," she said, beginning to weep. "I don't believe it."

"You must believe it."

"Do you know what tortures me?" she choked. "That I didn't stop him kissing me."

"I don't suppose he gave you any choice," Harlequin said gently. "Nobody could blame you."

"But I hate the memory. I never want to kiss another man, ever, in my life."

Harlequin touched her shoulder, but she pulled away and began to run from him. In the heavy dress and high heels she could not run fast, and he soon caught up with her.

"Wait, please – "

"Let me go," she wept. "I just want to hide away and never see anyone again."

"But you can't do that," he said, holding her firmly but gently. "You can't run away from the world, although you have enough courage to try. You must go on bravely, and find the man you truly love."

She could not speak, but she shook her head in despair. Harlequin put his fingers beneath her chin and lifted it so that he could look into her face.

"You are beautiful," he said. "I can see only your mouth, but it is lovely and I know the rest of you is the same. It's a mouth made to be kissed, and you must accept that, and not go through life remembering only that one man's kiss."

"Nothing can prevent that now," she said.

"Oh yes. I'm going to prevent it."

Before she could realise what he meant to do, Harlequin had lowered his head and pressed his lips against hers. After the first gasp of shock, Rona realised that this was very different from Lord Robert's kiss.

There was a gentleness about this man that was irresistible. His arms were strong, holding her against him as he moved his lips over hers with such beguiling tenderness that her very heart seemed to melt within her.

To think she might never have known this, might have wandered through the world forever, not knowing that this feeling could exist between a man and a woman, thinking that all men were like Lord Robert.

She was only half aware of her own hands moving to clasp him in return, to draw him closer, seeking a new beauty that she did not understand. Suddenly her arms were around his neck, and her spirit was soaring as she responded to his ardour.

It was mad, it was scandalous and unladylike. But it was also right. Everything in her was telling her that.

At last he released her. She looked up, wishing with all her heart that she could see his face now. She desperately needed to see it, to know if his feelings had been the same as hers. Her heart was beating wildly.

"What have you done?" she asked in wonder.

"I've made it impossible for you to think of him without remembering me," he said with a strange smile.

"Who are you?" she whispered. "I must know."

But he shook his head.

"It's better if you do not. We mustn't see each other's faces, and after tonight we can never meet again. I wish we could. I would like to remain close to you and protect you, but my path leads in another direction. I will always remember you."

"And I, you," she said, knowing that it was true.

How could she ever forget him, when he already lived inside her, in her memory, her heart and soul?

He kissed her again briefly, lightly, releasing her at once.

"Now we must return to the house," he said.

Taking her hand, he began to walk and soon they were among the lights. She could hear the sound of music and see couples dancing through the great windows. At any moment he would leave her and she must find a way to stop him. It was vital that she knew who he was.

On the stone steps he halted and said,

"You must go in alone, now."

"Wait," she implored, "Just one moment."

He shook his head, but before she could say more she heard a man's voice behind her.

"Hey there, Harlequin! It's Peter, isn't it?"

She whirled and saw a merry group of people some yards away, calling and waving in their direction.

"Hey, Peter – over here – "

She turned back to Harlequin, starting to say, "so your name is – ?"

But he had vanished.

CHAPTER THREE

"I am seriously displeased with you," Papa raged. "That a daughter of mine could display such rudeness, could show me up in front of everyone – how dare you leave without a word to me!"

"I left a message to say I'd gone home early, Papa," Rona said wearily.

If only her parents would leave her in peace. She had fled Westminster House, desperate to be alone and come home to bed. But then she had lain awake, listening for their return, knowing they would come straight to see her.

"How do you think it looked, leaving your fiancé alone like that?" her mother demanded.

"Mama, please don't call him my fiancé. I will not marry Lord Robert."

"You'll do as I say, my girl," her father snapped.

"He cares as little for me as I for him. He only wants your money. I heard him say so tonight."

He stared. "What are you talking about."

"I heard him tell someone – "

"Rubbish! You imagined it."

"Papa, I – "

"Not another word. Tomorrow I shall put the announcement in *The Times*."

She had thought the revelation of Lord Robert's true nature would be decisive, but now she saw that her parents were simply determined to block it out. And she could not tell more of the story without compromising Doreen.

When her parents had gone, her father in a rage, her mother in tears, Rona tossed and turned.

'I must escape,' she told herself. 'Or they'll march me up the aisle before I know what's happening. Then I'll spend the rest of my days married to a man I dislike and despise.

'But how can I flee? What can I do?' The questions seemed to throb in her head.

She finally fell asleep, and awoke very late next morning. When she came downstairs her parents had both left the house.

She went out into the garden and wandered among the flowers, wondering what was to become of her.

If only she could tell her parents everything, but that would include what had happened at the end of the evening. There were no words to describe the mysterious Harlequin, but she knew that his kiss would haunt her as long as she lived.

His purpose had been to wipe out the memory of Lord Robert's kiss, and he had succeeded more than he would ever know. Now she wanted no other embrace. In her heart she belonged to this one man.

Yet she did not even know who he was.

Except that his name was Peter.

But there were so many men in the world with that name, that it was no help.

Worse, she might never know his identity, for he had said they would not meet again.

She was overcome by despair at the thought that a magical door had been opened for her, only to be cruelly shut in her face.

Now the thought of marrying Lord Robert was more distasteful than ever.

'Never,' she said to herself. 'Never, never. Oh, I must get away from here! But how?'

Then, suddenly, she halted in her tracks as a memory came back to her.

The advertisement that she had read in the library last night, for a governess who could speak French and German.

This was the answer.

If she went abroad nobody could pressure her into marriage.

'But do I dare?' she thought. 'Yes. He said I must have courage, and I will.'

She began to run back to the house, determined to do something before her courage failed her. But when she reached the library she found the newspaper gone, replaced by today's copy.

"Oh no!" she cried.

"Can I help you, miss?"

It was Jenkins, the butler, who had just entered. She forced herself to sound calm.

"Jenkins, do you know where yesterday's *Times* is?"

"I have replaced it with today's copy, miss."

"Of course. But I want yesterday's. There – there was a report of a debate in the House of Lords that particularly interests me."

"In that case, I will obtain it for you, miss. Always assuming that the boot boy has not yet torn it up."

Luckily the boot boy was a little behind in his duties that morning, and the newspaper was retrieved without difficulty. Trying not to look too excited, Rona thanked Jenkins and hurried up to her room.

There it was, the advertisement she had seen the night before. If she hurried she might be in time.

She still possessed a rather dull coat and skirt which

she had worn during her last term at school, and kept because she thought they might be useful when it was raining. In fact she had never worn them again, but they were still in one of her extensive wardrobes.

Then she put on a hat from which she removed the decorations.

The final touch was her mother's reading glasses, which she hoped would make her look severe, and older. She was quite pleased with the result when she looked into the mirror. If she did not appear quite as old as she hoped, neither did she look like the beautiful young debutante that the world knew.

She slipped out into the street, and soon hailed a cab. In a few minutes they reached Oxford Street, where the agency was situated. She paid off the driver and hurried in.

Inside the agency she found an elderly woman seated at a large and rather high desk. In front of her was a small notice that said, *Miss Duncan.*

"What can I do for you?" she asked, rather sharply.

"I've come about the advertisement for a governess who speaks several languages," said Rona. She added, more firmly than she felt, "I think the situation would suit me."

"I doubt it," said Miss Duncan despondently. "It doesn't seem to suit anyone. It's for the Earl of Lancing's daughter. She left two schools because she wouldn't learn anything, and they were both glad to see her go. Rude and rebellious. The last three applicants left because she insulted them. I'm being honest with you because it's just a waste of time to send people there without warning them."

"Very well, you've warned me," said Rona. "Let me see what I can do."

"Name?" asked Miss Duncan.

"Rona Tr- Rona Johnson," amended Rona quickly.

Johnson had been her mother's maiden name.

"Very well, Miss Johnson. The Earl is usually at home in the morning, so if you go now you'll probably find him there. Here's the address, in Berkeley Square. If you show Lord Lancing this card, he'll know that you've come from us."

Outside, she hailed another cab and as they drove to Berkeley Square, Rona mused on the opportunity that had so unexpectedly opened up to her.

'If I can stay away for perhaps a month or so, it will make Papa realise that I am serious in refusing to marry Lord Robert. Perhaps, then, I can come back.'

She prayed to all the angels in heaven to guide her into doing and saying the right things so that the rebellious girl would accept her.

The Earl's house in Berkeley Square was very big and impressive. In answer to her knock the door was opened by an elderly butler. When she explained why she had come, he nodded and stood back for her to pass.

While she waited for him to inform the Earl, she looked around her at some very fine pictures and valuable furniture. At the sound of his returning footsteps, she opened her handbag and slipped her mother's glasses on to her nose.

"His Lordship will see you now."

She followed him down the passage until he opened a door and showed her into a well-furnished and, she thought, attractive study. There were several bookcases in the room. Their owner was sitting at a very impressive desk on which there were gold-topped inkpots and gold candlesticks.

"Miss Johnson, my Lord."

A man, who seemed to be in his forties rose from his desk and came towards her. He was heavily built with a weary, gentle face and hair that was just beginning to turn grey.

"How do you do," he said. "I understand you have come from Miss Duncan."

"Yes, she told me you were looking for a governess for your daughter who must speak several European languages."

The Earl smiled.

"That is true. Now suppose we sit down and you tell me how experienced you are."

Rona knew by the expression in his eyes that he was surprised to see her so young, so she quickly chose a chair with its back to the window, hoping that he would not see her face too clearly. He watched her curiously.

"I suppose Miss Duncan told you that my daughter, Alice, has been rather difficult where other governesses have been concerned. But I'm continually called abroad, and would like to take her with me. My wife is unfortunately dead."

"It said in the advertisement she is sixteen."

"Yes," the Earl replied. "Actually she will soon be seventeen. You may think I've left it rather late to trouble about her education, but she was much upset by her mother's death four years ago. She ran away from one school after another because she wanted to be with me. I can't blame her for that, but I hoped her rebellion would pass. Unfortunately, it didn't. Now I need to make up lost time." He frowned. "But you are very young."

"Then I'm just what you need," Rona said quickly. "Because I'm nearer her age than I suspect the others have been, I will be more successful. Let me talk to her, and see if I can win her confidence."

"And if you do, can you be ready to leave for France tomorrow?"

Rona took a deep breath.

"Yes," she said firmly.

"Very well, I'll take you to meet her."

She followed him out into the corridor and upstairs to the second floor.

"Alice has her own sitting room up here," he said. "It used to be the nursery."

The room turned out to be large and attractive with windows looking out over the square. Sitting beside one of them was a very pretty girl. She had fair hair which fell over her shoulders, and a pale face. She looked defiant, but also Rona thought, unhappy.

As Alice turned round to see who was coming into the room, a big smile broke over her face.

"Papa!" she said in delight, running to hug him.

He embraced her back. It was clear that there was a very strong affection between them. But Rona also guessed that he was alarmed by his daughter, and did not know what to do with her.

"I have here a lady who is very anxious to meet you," he began. "Her name is Miss Johnson."

The girl saw Rona.

"Oh, not another governess!" she groaned. "The last one when she left told me that I was impossible. I thought that would be the end of them."

"This one is different," her father said. "I want you to talk to her and then we'll see if she'll come with us when we leave England tomorrow."

The girl, without moving, was staring at Rona. Then she said to her father,

"I don't want her," she said firmly. "I want to go abroad with you alone without a tiresome governess trailing about behind us."

Rona thought of the dire retribution that would have fallen on her if she had dared speak to her father like that.

But the Earl seemed helpless to control his child.

"Alice, darling," he said after a moment, "Please be reasonable."

Alice's answer was to stamp her foot and turn her back on them.

Lord Lancing gave Rona a helpless shrug.

It was time she took charge.

"I think, my Lord, that I should like to talk to your daughter alone."

The Earl looked at her in surprise. Then he gave a brief nod and walked from the room shutting the door behind him.

Rona and Alice eyed each other.

Then Rona said lightly,

"It must be a bore for you, having to interview tiresome women like me."

This approach was evidently new because Alice was taken aback, but she recovered herself enough to say defiantly.

"Yes, it is."

"I'm only curious about why you so dislike learning foreign languages."

She had moved a little closer. Now she slipped off her glasses, so that Alice could see how near they were in age.

"I hate the women who keep telling me that I am ignorant," said Alice sulkily.

Rona laughed.

"I don't blame you for that," she said. "I know exactly what they're like. When I was at school I used to daydream through a lot of my lessons."

"But you have come here wanting to teach me, and I hate it. The others have tried and failed. Why should you succeed?"

Rona thought quickly. She needed a new approach, one that would take Alice by surprise, and intrigue her.

"I wonder what they taught you," she said, apparently casual. "You are very pretty and Frenchmen love pretty women. What are you going to say when one of them says, '*Vous êtes tres jolie,*' and tries to kiss you?"

The girl stared at her.

"Do you think they'll say that?" she asked.

"Of course," Rona replied. "And you must have an answer, otherwise they'll all be trying to kiss you, and your father will be shocked."

"Supposing someone did want to kiss me? What do I answer?"

"If you knew French you would say: '*Merci Monsieur, mais, non, non, non!*' I suppose you know that means, no, no, no."

Alice considered. Rona could see that she was torn between fascination and maintaining her defiance.

"Suppose I wanted to kiss him?" she asked after a moment.

"That is different altogether," Rona replied. "But it would be a great mistake to encourage him too soon. He'll want to flirt with you because you are so pretty, so you must have a clever and amusing way of answering him and making him behave himself."

Alice regarded her, with her head on one side.

"None of the others talked to me like this," she mused.

"Maybe nobody had ever tried to kiss them?" Rona suggested. "Perhaps, without realising it, they were trying to make you as dull as themselves."

"Am I really attractive?"

"You are very pretty," Rona replied. "Whether you are attractive is a different thing. It depends on how charming

41

you can be, how exciting, and how interesting."

"My last governess said girls aren't supposed to be interesting. She was always trying to shut me up."

"She was probably afraid that you'd say something she couldn't answer," said Rona. "I'm a little afraid of that myself."

Unexpectedly Alice laughed.

"No you aren't," she cried. "You can't fool me. You're not afraid of anything. I like you. Will you teach me to be like you?"

"There are better things to be than like me. I'll tell you how to make yourself attractive and delightful to everyone you meet. That's what we all want to be, but sometimes it's very difficult."

Rona added, apparently as an afterthought, "Of course, you'll need to buy a lot of new clothes in Paris."

Alice looked at her impishly.

"I don't believe you are really a governess at all," she said.

Rona glanced towards the door to make sure it was safely closed.

"I'll tell you the truth, but you must swear not to tell anyone else."

"I promise," Alice replied.

"Very well," Rona said. "I need to escape London because I'm being pressured to marry a man I don't like."

Alice's eyes widened. "How thrilling!"

"But of course if you don't want me, and won't work with me – " She spread her hands expressively.

"I'll work with you if you talk to me as you do now," Alice promised. "All the others just tried to teach me about verbs and adjectives."

"There's more to life than verbs and adjectives," Rona agreed solemnly. "In another year or so you'll be getting proposals of marriage, and you'll have to know how to refuse in such a way that they know you mean it – " She shuddered suddenly as memories came back to her, and for a moment she stared into space.

"Miss Johnson?" Alice held out her hand. "What's the matter?"

"Nothing," Rona said, giving herself a mental shake. "What I meant was that you must refuse charmingly, so that the man doesn't become angry, but continues to be your slave, while he begs you to change your mind."

Alice's eyes were shining.

"That's the sort of thing I want to learn," she said.

"Perhaps we should keep it to ourselves for a while," Rona suggested. "Otherwise your father may think I'm teaching you the wrong things and send me away."

"He won't do that," Alice said cheerfully. "He'll be so relieved to have a governess that I like."

Rona laughed.

"Stop being such a little tyrant," she said. "If you're going to be a charming young lady, start by treating your father more kindly."

Alice considered. It was clearly a new idea to her that fathers needed to be treated kindly.

"I'll think about it," she said at last.

"That will do for the moment. Now I must go to see him, and tell him we've reached an agreement."

Suddenly Alice dropped her grown up ways and became a child again, throwing her arms about Rona, and hugging her as though she would prevent her leaving.

"You have come to save me when I was feeling desperate," she said. "If you go home to fetch your luggage, do you promise to come back this afternoon? I can't help thinking that I'm dreaming and suddenly you will disappear."

"I promise to return as soon as I've collected my things from home."

She bent down and kissed Alice on the cheek. Then she ran down the stairs and back to the room where the Earl was sitting at his desk. When Rona entered the room he looked up.

"Well?" he asked.

"Alice and I are delighted with each other, and if you engage me I'm going back now to fetch my luggage."

"Excellent!" exclaimed the Earl. "Now, about your salary."

"Let's discuss it when I come back," Rona replied. "I have a lot of packing to do and I have promised your daughter I'll return as quickly as I can."

She hurried away as she finished speaking and the Earl stared at the closed door.

Then he put his hand up to his forehead. He wasn't used to young women who flew out of the door before he said they could go, and he certainly was not used to a governess who shrugged aside any mention of money.

At least she was different, he thought hopefully.

*

Luck was with Rona. She arrived home to find her parents still out. If she acted fast she had enough time to leave without discovery.

Her maid was out as well, which left her to pack for herself, but meant one less pair of curious eyes.

She took some of her best clothes, in case she needed to look smart when they were abroad. At the same time she was wise enough to put in some of her more simple dresses, so that she could occasionally look like a governess.

Then she sat down at the writing-table in her bedroom and wrote a letter to her father.

Darling Mama and Papa, please forgive me for leaving like this, but I simply cannot do as you wish and marry Lord Robert. Don't worry about me. I am safe.

I love you both, and I will miss you, but you will understand that for the moment I cannot see Lord Robert.

Your very affectionate daughter, Rona

'There is one thing at any rate I will teach her,' Rona told herself, 'and that is that men can be very deceptive and before one promises them anything, one must know exactly who they are and what they feel in their own hearts.'

She put the letter in an envelope.

Then, picking up one of her cases she took it downstairs and told the footman to bring down the others.

There were, in fact, four large cases and a vanity case which contained some of her jewellery.

She left the letter she had written to her father on his writing-desk, while the footman was bringing down her luggage, and another summoned a cab. When she was ready to leave, she said loudly to the driver,

"Take me to Kensington station."

She knew that instruction would be repeated to her father when he returned.

The cab set off. When they had almost reached Oxford Street she called to the driver, "I've changed my mind. Take me to Berkeley Square."

As soon as she arrived she knew they were waiting for her. The door was opened immediately. She ran upstairs to the sitting room. As soon as she opened the door, Alice gave a cry of joy and excitement and ran towards her.

"You have come! You have come!" she cried. "I was

afraid it was just a dream and I would never see you again."

"I promised to return, and here I am."

"But people don't always keep their promises," said Alice. "Mama promised never to leave me, but then she died."

There was a forlorn note in her voice that told Rona all she needed to know about the girl's loneliness.

"But you must not blame your mother for that," she said gently. "Things happen that are beyond our control. We will talk about this later. First, where am I to sleep tonight?"

"In my room," Alice said eagerly. "While we're away they'll prepare a proper room for you."

A truckle bed had been moved into Alice's pleasant room, but it proved to be rather uncomfortable when Rona tried it.

"No, I'm sleeping there," Alice said quickly. "You're having my bed."

It was almost as though she was afraid her new friend might take offence and leave. Rona smiled, feeling pleased that she was already winning Alice's confidence.

A message came from the Earl to say that he hoped they would both dine with him that evening. Rona put on her plainest dress and the glasses. She did not intend to wear them for ever, but it would be safer to look dowdy until they were in France.

To complete the effect she brushed her hair straight back, so that it lay flat against her head, and fixed it into a neat bun at the nape of her neck.

She hardly knew the person who looked back at her from the mirror. She had braced herself for the glasses, the dreary clothes, and the even drearier hair.

There was something else. This pale woman with the set face and disillusioned eyes was a stranger, and yet herself. She had been born some time in the last few hours, and now she would not go away.

She was the person who would be living her life in future. And she made Rona realise that she had no idea what that future held.

But she would face it with courage.

Harlequin had told her that she could do so and following his precepts was now all that she had left of him.

CHAPTER FOUR

Most of Alice's clothes had been packed, but Rona went through the few that were left and chose a blue dress that was pretty and simple. Then she brushed the girl's hair until it shone, leaving it to flow freely down to her shoulders.

At last they were ready to go downstairs.

The Earl looked up as they came in, and she thought she caught a look of surprise on his face as he saw her, looking even more drab than before.

"Ladies," he said, "shall we go in to dinner?"

As Alice went ahead he detained Rona a moment.

"I think I understand what you're doing," he said. "But it doesn't work."

"Sir?"

"Nothing is going to make you look plain, Miss Johnson," he told her with a hint of a smile.

"I am only trying to look like a governess," she said with a hint of severity.

He gave her his arm. "Let us go in."

In truth Rona was on hot coals lest her parents should find her before she could leave the country. How lucky that they were leaving so soon.

In the meantime she must do all she could to convince the Earl that she was the right person for his daughter.

Over dinner it was she who kept the conversation going, sensing that father and daughter, for all their affection,

48

had very little notion of what to say to each other. Skilfully she drew him out to talk about France, and prompted Alice into asking him questions. This was not hard as the girl was now in a fever of anticipation.

The Earl and his daughter were soon chattering happily together, and Rona regarded them with satisfaction.

"Papa, Miss Johnson says I will need lots of new dresses, and she will help me choose them."

"Indeed? And who will help me pay for them? Don't look like that, my darling, I'm only joking."

The conversation took a different turn. Alice began talking about her mother, sounding a little wistful.

"We were so happy then, weren't we, Papa?"

The Earl nodded.

"And sometimes Uncle Peter would come and stay with us. Oh, Miss Johnson, is something the matter?"

"No," she said quickly. "I simply dropped my spoon into the bowl. Go on with what you were saying."

"Uncle Peter is Mama's brother, and he's wonderful. I wish we saw him more often."

"He visits us when he can," her father said. "But you know him – here, there and everywhere."

"You said you were going to bar him from the house," Alice said.

"I did not," said the Earl, sounding harassed. "In a moment of exasperation I said I *ought* to bar him from the house. But I've never done so."

To Rona he added,

"While Alice is so fond of that reprobate, I could never bar him."

"But why is he a reprobate, sir?" Rona asked, amused.

"Oh, he lives a rather wild, undisciplined life," said the Earl vaguely.

"Lots of ladies," Alice confided gravely.

"Alice!" exclaimed the Earl, scandalised.

"But Papa, it's no secret. Last time Uncle Peter was staying with us, this terribly angry man came to the door. I could hear the row from upstairs – "

"You didn't hear anything," said her father, moved to firmness at last. "Miss Johnson I beg you not to think too badly of us. My brother-in-law is a notorious flirt, but that's the worst you can say of him. Now Alice, that's enough. You should go to bed early, because if you oversleep tomorrow I shall leave you behind."

"*Papa!*" Alice squealed.

"Goodnight, my Lord," said Rona, laughing.

When he was alone the Earl went to sit in his library with a brandy, and think over the events of the day, and in particular to think about Miss Johnson.

'One of the most extraordinary young women I've ever met,' he mused, with a smile on his broad, kindly face. 'She certainly swept through this place like a whirlwind. Ah well, it's time I was going to bed too, otherwise I'll set a poor example tomorrow morning.'

As he rose from his seat, he heard the sound of the front door bell.

'Who can that be at this time of night?' he wondered.

He heard the door being opened, Benson giving a pleased exclamation, then the sound of a familiar voice. The Earl grinned. The next moment he was in the hall, advancing on the tall young man, his hand outstretched.

"Peter! By all that's wonderful! Come in my boy!"

The young man grinned back and embraced the Earl heartily.

"Giles! You thought you'd got rid of me, didn't you?" he cried. "But, like a bad penny, I always turn up."

"Thank goodness for that!" the Earl said sincerely, for despite his strictures he was fond of his late wife's infamous brother.

"Benson, bring some more brandy to the library," the Earl called. "And tell the housekeeper to make up Mr. Carlton's usual room."

When the two men were settled in deep leather armchairs, the Earl surveyed his young brother-in-law with satisfaction.

"Talk of the devil," he said. "We were discussing you over dinner tonight?"

"We?"

"Alice was telling her new governess all about you. Including 'ladies'."

"Alice doesn't know *all* about me and ladies," said Peter in alarm. "At least, I hope she doesn't. Anyway, I'm a reformed character."

"Again?" the Earl enquired.

They both laughed.

Peter leaned back against the leather, closing his eyes, and the Earl thought that nobody could blame the women who sighed for him. He was ridiculously handsome, with a tall, lithe figure and elegant movements. His face was lean, with fine features and a wide, mobile mouth that laughed readily.

"Alice will be sad not to see more of you," said the Earl. "You know what a favourite you are with her. But we're going to France tomorrow morning."

Peter yawned and opened his eyes. "I could always tag along," he suggested sleepily. "If you could bear to have me."

"You know better than to say that. Of course you can come, and be welcome. We're staying with the Thierre family, and I know they're fond of you."

"Tell me about the new governess."

"She's extraordinary. I've never known anyone like her. She's much too young and pretty, although she tries to pretend she isn't."

"What does Alice think? I remember she was being a bit difficult about governesses."

"That's the extraordinary thing. Alice loves her, and I must admit that she handles the child very cleverly. At dinner tonight she was telling her all about Paris, not the monuments, like other governesses, but the dress shops."

"So Alice was listening to that?" said Peter with a grin.

"With both ears."

"Then you should watch out for your wallet."

"I've already said goodbye to my wallet. Miss Johnson has promised Alice that I'm going to buy her a wardrobe full of French fashions. And she kept slipping in French words and phrases, so that Alice had to ask her what she meant. I think she's beginning to want to learn the language."

"She sounds like a paragon, this governess. I can't wait to meet her."

"You will behave yourself like a gentleman," said the Earl quickly. "I don't want her driven out because you tried to flirt with her."

"My dear fellow, I never flirt with governesses. I consider it unchivalrous."

"Good. Mind you, she's not like a governess at all. She's definitely a lady, and a very cultured one. I can't help wondering why someone so pretty and clever has to earn her own living."

Peter sat up, suddenly alert.

"Pretty," he mused.

"Yes, I told you."

"You've told me several times. Is there more to this than meets the eye?"

"I don't know what you mean." But the Earl coughed self-consciously.

"You ought to marry again, I've always said so. I know you were devoted to Valerie, but she's been dead for four years."

"I've only known this young lady a few hours," said the Earl, sounding harassed.

"Sometimes that's all it takes," Peter said reflectively. "Or even less. All right, old boy, I won't hound you about her, but I hope you will be very happy."

"Peter – "

"I'll shut up! Not another word."

"Get yourself to bed," the Earl growled. "We all have to be up early."

*

Rona was downstairs ahead of Alice next morning as she wanted to have a private word with the Earl. She found him already at the table in the breakfast room. He looked up and smiled at her.

"Good morning," he said. "You are very punctual, and that's something I always appreciate in a woman."

"My father was furious if anyone kept him waiting," Rona replied, "so I am well trained at being on time."

"That reminds me, I haven't asked you who your father is, or where he lives."

Rona had helped herself to the eggs and bacon which were on the sideboard. As she put her plate down on the table, she said,

"A new world is opening its arms to me. I want to

53

think about the future and not the past."

The Earl gave a rueful smile.

"In other words," he said, "you're telling me to mind my own business. Very well, because you're such a success with my daughter I'll try to do everything as you wish, and not be over curious."

Rona did not speak and after a moment he went on, "I realise that your name is not the one you were born with."

She stiffened and stared at him.

"Why do you say that?" she asked.

"Because, my dear, I saw your luggage in the hall and there are different initials on two of the cases to the name you have given me."

Rona frowned.

"That was very stupid of me," she said. "I forgot when I collected my luggage at home that the cases once belonged to somebody else, and still bear that person's initials."

She held her breath, hoping that he would be satisfied with this explanation.

"Well, we won't talk about it, at the moment," the Earl answered with a smile that made her sure he did not believe her. "If you want to be mysterious of course I won't spoil things."

"Thank you very much and I will try not to forget it," Rona replied.

The Earl laughed. That certainly was not the reply he had expected. But she was so original and enchanting that he was willing to tolerate much from her that he would not have accepted from anyone else.

"I came down early," said Rona, "because I want to ask you to say nothing about lessons. Of course I shall be teaching Alice, but discreetly. I'm trying to make her want to learn."

"Yes I saw that last night. Don't worry. In fact, I have something to tell you as well. We have an extra person – "

He broke off as his face lit up at the sight of his daughter dancing into the room.

"There you are," he said as she hugged him. "I was just going to tell Miss Johnson about the surprise."

"Oh, lovely! What is it?"

"Not what? Who?"

"Me," said a voice behind Alice, and they all turned to see a smiling young man.

Alice gave a shriek of pleasure and ran into his arms, crying, "Uncle Peter!"

He lifted her off her feet and swung her around. "How's my favourite girl?"

"You're back," she cried when he had set her down again. "I'm so glad."

"You're so grown up," he said.

The Earl spoke quietly to Rona.

"That's Peter Carlton, my brother-in-law, just back from his travels. I wasn't expecting him for another month. You may remember that we were talking about him last night."

When she did not reply he looked at her intently.

"Miss Johnson?"

She seemed to wake up from a dream.

"I'm sorry, my Lord."

"What is it? You look as if you've seen a ghost."

"No – no, not at all. Just a momentary impression. An illusion. Nothing."

Alice was pulling her uncle over to Rona.

"Uncle Peter, this is Miss Johnson who's going to be

my new governess, and she's so wonderfully different from the others. It's like magic."

"So you are a magician, Miss Johnson?" said Peter Carlton, holding out his hand to Rona in a frank, attractive manner.

"You are too kind, sir." Miss Johnson took his hand, but only for a moment, and did not meet his eyes.

Peter was regarding her in some bewilderment. Was this the woman whose beauty had so impressed his brother that he had continually alluded to it the night before? Well, she might be pretty, but it was hard to tell when she would not raise her head, and all he could see clearly was a dowdy hairstyle and a pair of glasses.

"She is like a fairy who has come into our lives and cast a spell over everything," Alice insisted.

"Are you really a fairy, Miss Johnson?" Peter asked in a warm, semi-playful tone. It came from his kind heart, and usually put nervous employees at their ease, which was his intention.

But instead of smiling at him this iron maiden (as he was beginning to think of her) merely said,

"That's just Miss Alice's way of talking, sir."

"Uncle Peter, Papa says you are coming with us to Paris," Alice exclaimed.

"Unless you object."

In answer Alice gave him an elegant little curtsy, and said, "to be sure, sir, your company will be very agreeable."

Peter laughed and gave her a bow. Thankful that his attention was no longer on her, Rona let out her breath. Her heart was beating wildly at what had just happened.

It was absurd, of course, to imagine any likeness between this man and Harlequin. He was tall and had the same name, but that was all. The rest was just her fancy.

All she needed, she thought, was a moment to pull herself together.

"Everybody have some breakfast," the Earl said heartily. "We must be going soon."

"Hurry, I don't want to be left behind," said Alice. "I do so want lots of new French clothes."

"Well, I dare say you will contrive to get what you want," said the Earl wryly. "And whatever it costs me, I don't mind if it makes you happy."

"Now that's a very pretty speech," Rona said. "I think to make your father happy, you must thank him for it in French."

Alice laughed.

"*Merci beaucoup, Papa,*" she said.

Her father bowed his head and his eyes were twinkling.

Rona knew that he was thinking that no other governess would have obtained those words from his daughter. Alice had spoken not only as if she was ordered to do so, but with all sincerity.

"As you are so polite," he said aloud to his daughter, "I will say *merci beaucoup*, for your kindness and add, *tu es tres chic,* and I hope you understand that."

"Of course I do," Alice replied. "I think by the time we get back from Paris, with Miss Johnson teaching me, I will speak even better French than you."

"That will be the day, and you will then have champagne for supper," her father answered. "You must remind me if you have earned it by the time we come home."

"You will be surprised," Alice said.

The Earl did not answer, he merely looked at Rona and smiled. She smiled back, understanding that he was thanking her.

Peter observed them both quietly.

Rona felt that she was quite herself again now. The brief fancy had passed, and she could speak to Peter Carlton without losing her composure.

*

The last half hour before their departure was torture for Rona. At any moment she was sure that her father would arrive. But at last they were in the Earl's carriage, on the way to the station to catch the train for Dover.

When at last the train was finally moving, the men sat and talked in the First Class compartment, while Alice and Rona stood in the corridor watching the countryside go by.

'It can't be him,' Rona thought, 'and I must stop brooding about it. He showed no sign of recognising me. But then, how could he? That white wig I wore at the ball completely covered my hair, and the mask covered most of my face.'

Then they reached Dover and she had no further chance to speculate, because there was so much to be done.

For the short journey across the water to Calais the Earl had reserved two rooms, one with a bed in case anyone was seasick. The other was a private sitting room.

At Rona's suggestion she and Alice stayed on deck to watch the ship put to sea.

"I always think this is so exciting," she said.

"My last governess wouldn't get on a ship," said Alice. "She said she couldn't understand why it didn't sink. She was scared of trains too. She called them 'nasty new-fangled things'."

"Some people are scared of anything new," Rona agreed. "But you're young, and it's right for you to be interested in new things. Too many people say, 'we have managed without that before and we can manage without it now'."

Alice was thoughtful.

"As I am a woman, do I have to be brave?" she asked at last.

"Of course," Rona replied. "Men think courage is just for them, but it's the women who praise them and make them feel they must go out and look for new ideas, new ways of travel, and eventually, new ways of thinking. It's up to you, as a woman, to make the men try to invent new things to please you."

"Please me?" Alice questioned.

"All women have, since the beginning of time, inspired men with their desires," Rona told her.

"I think I see what you mean," Alice mused. "A woman is too feeble to do it herself, but she can urge a man to do it for her."

"That's right. Then when the man comes back with something new, whether it is small or large, you must tell him he's wonderful."

"But perhaps I could have done it better, or quicker?"

"You must never say so," Rona warned her. "A man must be praised."

"Even if I thought of it first?"

"Then you must let him think *he* thought of it first."

"But suppose I think up a way to make a better ship?"

"Don't forget it has to be the man who will make the ship," said Rona wryly, "the man who will get the credit for it and the man who will eventually steer it."

"That's not fair," Alice complained. "If we think of it they ought to praise us, and name the ship after us. What do we get?"

"You get his admiration. He thinks you're wonderful even though he forgets it's your brain which has inspired him."

Alice mused for a while.

"That's really rather clever," she said. "If a man wants a good teacher he has to find a woman, like you, to inspire him."

"Not necessarily like me," Rona said.

"No, I think Alice is right," said a voice behind them.

Turning, they saw Peter, regarding them with an amused smile.

"You've been eavesdropping," Alice accused him.

"Yes, and I've heard some very interesting things." He strolled forward and leaned on the rail, standing next to Rona. "So that's how the trick is worked, eh?"

"Oh Miss Johnson," said Alice in dismay, "It's no good. Now he knows the secret it won't work."

Peter cocked an eyebrow at Rona, as though intrigued to know how she would react. Smiling, she said,

"Don't worry, Alice. They've known the secret since the dawn of time, but it still works."

"But how can it?"

"Because men believe what it suits them to believe," said Rona. "You can always rely on that."

Peter roared with laughter.

"It's true, I can't deny it," he said at once.

"Oh look," said Alice, "there's poor Papa. He looks as if he might be feeling seasick."

She darted away, but when Rona would have followed her Peter put out a hand to detain her.

"She doesn't need you if she's with her father," he said. "Stay and tell me about these curious lessons you're teaching my niece."

"You were not meant to hear."

"In case we learn the secret? But, as you rightly

pointed out, we've always known." He grinned in a way she found delightful. "It's interesting to discover that women teach each other how to make fools of us men. I thought it was something you were all born knowing."

His droll manner made her smile.

"We are," she said, "but it helps to refine it. And it isn't all men. Only those stupid and lazy enough to want to believe the lie."

"You relieve my mind ma'am. So any man who wants to, may console himself with the thought that he's one of the intelligent few that women don't secretly despise. Except that that very belief may only prove that she's making him the biggest fool of all?"

"Ah!" she said with a pretended sigh. "And there was I, hoping to delude you."

They laughed together. When the laughter faded they stood for a moment, leaning on the rail, side by side, staring out over the waves.

Rona knew she should end this conversation. She had resolved to avoid him. But she had never before met a man who engaged her in such delicious verbal duelling, and the pleasure was intoxicating. She would avoid him later, she told herself.

"I think you're a very clever woman, ma'am," he said. "And the way you've won my niece's confidence is the cleverest thing of all."

"People told me she was difficult. I don't think so. I think she's just unhappy and lonely and needs a friend."

"I think so too," he said seriously. "And I'm glad she's found one in you. I should like to call you my friend, also."

He held out his hand, and she shook it.

Then a change seemed to come over him. Instead of releasing her hand, he looked down at it, lying in his own, so small and dainty. For a moment he was quite still, as though struck by a thought.

A tremor went through him. Rona felt it distinctly through the pressure of his hand.

"Perhaps we should rejoin the others," he said.

"Yes." She scarcely knew what she said. She felt as though a light had gone out.

The four of them spent the rest of the time down below, eating a light lunch, and soon they were in Calais.

There was much to do, supervising the luggage with the help of Alice's maid, and Rona found she had no time to think.

But then they were on the train from Calais to Paris, with miles and miles to think.

Now she was pursued by thoughts she would rather avoid. Questions to which she did not know the answer.

Was he Harlequin? Had he too had a frisson of memory?

But when they reached Paris, his manner was brisk and businesslike and she decided that she must have imagined everything.

At last they were drawing away from the railway station in a carriage. As they sat back in the comfortable seats the Earl said,

"I wonder which of us is the most excited at being in Paris."

"That's me," Alice replied, "because Miss Johnson tells me I am going to find fascinating things in Paris that I've never seen before."

"And of course," said Rona, "you will be told all about it – in French."

The Earl smiled.

"I shall enjoy that. I'm looking forward to this visit

too, because in the past I've been alone."

"And I too am looking forward to it," said Rona. "I'm sure things have changed since I was last here."

"So you've been here before?" the Earl asked. "You didn't tell me that."

"I think, to be honest, you took it for granted," Rona replied. "I love France, especially Paris, and it's such a pleasure to return to it."

The Earl looked at her.

"You are full of surprises, Miss Johnson," he said.

"I think Alice will find it as exciting as I did," Rona said, adding with meaning, "especially when we go shopping."

The Earl laughed.

"That's what I'm afraid of."

Alice clapped her hands and gave a cry.

"Papa, you are not to be mean, and I will buy you a lovely present. And I'm going to learn to be *a woman of distinction*, like Miss Johnson. And you will be very proud of me."

"Miss Johnson, I'm amazed," said the Earl. "How have you transformed this imp in so little time?"

"That's a secret," Rona answered, with a smile at Alice.

Peter Carlton had been listening to all this with interest. Now he spoke to the Earl.

"You know, old fellow, I think you're soon going to get the biggest shock of your life.

"If all shocks are as pleasant as this," said the Earl, "I'm going to look forward to them."

CHAPTER FIVE

Lord Lancing's party was to stay with Monsieur Armand Thierre and his family in their elegant home on the Champs Elysees.

While Monsieur Thierre had no title he was one of the most influential men, not only in Paris but anywhere on the continent. He was an international banker of vast wealth and influence. He held no government post, but his quietly uttered words were heeded.

Neither he nor his wife displayed any dismay at the extra numbers added to the party, and greeted Peter like an old friend, as he was.

When the hostess bent to kiss Alice, she said in French, "It is very kind of you to have me here."

She said it slowly and carefully, just as Rona had taught her.

Madame Thierre was delighted.

Watching the Earl, Rona was pleased to see him gasp in pleasure and astonishment.

Footmen were already carrying their luggage upstairs. They followed and found themselves in a large elegant bedroom. It might have belonged to a Princess, Rona thought, looking around at the gilt mirrors and paintings on the ceiling.

For a moment she forgot her difficult situation in the happiness of being in Paris again. Then she set to work, directing the maid who was beginning to unpack.

For the first time Alice saw the clothes that had reposed in Rona's trunks, and her eyes widened at the fashionable garments.

"Oh, I like that so much," she said at a soft pink dress that appeared. "How lucky you are. I'm so tired of dressing like a schoolgirl."

"You won't be a schoolgirl very much longer," Rona promised her, reaching into the trunk for another dress, of delicate blue silk.

There was a knock on the door. Alice danced over and opened it, to find her father standing there.

"Oh, Papa, it's so beautiful." She took his hand and pulled him into the room. "It's such a lovely house, and what I've seen of Paris is lovely, and my room is lovely, and everything is lovely."

He laughed at her excitement.

"I'm glad you like it, darling. Do you think you can be on your best behaviour for a formal dinner tonight?" His eyes twinkled. "Or had we better not risk it?"

"Oh please Papa. I'll be good."

"It's up to Miss Johnson."

Rona looked up from one of her trunks with an evening gown in her hands. "Sir?"

"If Alice comes to dinner, you must come too, to keep an eye on her. And wear that pretty blue dress you're holding."

She had just been thinking regretfully that in her character as governess she could not risk the blue dress. The Earl seemed to read her thoughts for he said.

"These are very elegant people. You must do me credit. And so must Alice."

"Very well, my Lord."

"I'll collect you both just before the reception starts."

"Excuse me," said Rona, "but I don't think Alice is quite ready for a grown up reception. Let me bring her down just for the meal."

"Very well. Whatever you think is proper. Oh, and by the way – don't wear your glasses tonight."

Rona quietly agreed, and the Earl went out, smiling to himself, for he thought he had handled that well.

When they dressed for dinner Rona decided to take a small risk. The Earl had said Alice must do him credit, so Rona allowed her to wear the pink gown that she had admired. It was fashionable but simple, and Alice was delighted.

Rona dressed the girl's hair herself, taking it up but not allowing the style to be too elaborate.

"There," she said, at last. "Now you look what you are. A beautiful young girl, on the edge of discovering that the world is yours."

"Listen," said Alice. "I hear wheels."

Looking out of the window they saw the first carriages driving up to the front door.

"Can't we go to the reception?" Alice pleaded.

"No, but we can go out onto the landing and watch them arrive."

They slipped out and leaned over the rail to watch gorgeously dressed men and woman swirl into the hall.

"Paris fashions," Alice breathed ecstatically.

"We'll get some for you," Rona promised.

"And some for you. But you are already so gorgeous that all the men will be in love with you."

Rona laughed.

"Now, why would I want all the men to be in love with me? What would I do with them? What matters is to have *the one* in love with you."

"Which one?" Alice asked, puzzled.

"The one your own heart has chosen, because only his love counts. When you've found him you have found everything in life that is important. Sometimes you have to be patient, but when the time comes, you mustn't be afraid to take any risk for your love."

"Is that what you did?" Alice asked earnestly.

"I – we weren't talking about me."

"But perhaps we should," said a voice behind them.

They turned to see Peter Carlton there, regarding them with a look of wicked amusement in his eyes.

"Mr. Carlton," Rona said crossly, "that is the second time you have crept up on a private conversation that I was having with your niece. It is most impolite to eavesdrop."

"But that's how you learn the really interesting things," he said outrageously. "After all, as you say, she *is* my niece. Naturally I want to know whether you're teaching her the right lessons – about propriety, and so forth."

"But how would you recognise propriety?" she demanded. "Since I am quite certain that you don't know the difference."

"Yes, teacher. No, teacher," he said drolly. "I take it that I'm now at the bottom of the class."

He was teasing her she knew, but for some reason she was angry with him. She felt, unreasonably, that he had no right to seem so like Harlequin, and yet not *be* Harlequin.

"You can stay there and hear me give Alice a lesson in propriety right this minute," she said stiffly.

"What?" Alice asked in alarm.

"Alice, you must always remember that it is grossly improper to listen to people's private conversations. You must never do so, or associate with those who indulge in this reprehensible practice."

His eyes danced. "So now I'm reprehensible. Miss Johnson, have I done something to offend you?"

"I've just finished telling you that you have. Were you not listening?"

"Ah, but I didn't mean just now. I meant – in general, are you angry with me? If so, I'll abase myself in sackcloth and ashes."

"Please do not be absurd," she told him coolly.

"What are sackcloth and ashes?" Alice asked innocently.

"You will find them in the Bible," Rona told her. "We will study it until it's time to go down to dinner."

She swept her charge back into the bedroom, glad to escape Peter Carlton's troubling humour, and his equally troubling good looks. In his white tie and evening attire he looked far too handsome.

"Is Uncle Peter an improper person?" Alice enquired when they were alone.

"I'm beginning to think he is."

"Because of his ladies?"

"Alice, this is not a suitable topic of conversation. We will talk of something else, if you please."

"Never mind, we'll see one tonight," said Alice.

"One what?"

"One of his ladies. Papa told me all about it. There's a Russian Countess coming to dinner. But I don't understand how she can be a Countess when she isn't married to anyone."

"Russian titles are different from ours," Rona explained. "In Russia, if a man is a Count then so are his sons, and his daughters are Countesses."

"It sounds very confusing."

"I agree."

"Monsieur Thierre invited the Countess Rostoya at the last minute because Uncle Peter specially asked him to. Isn't that exciting?"

"Enthralling," Rona agreed.

An hour later the Earl came for them. Like Peter he was in a white tie and tails. He looked sturdier and more imposing than his brother-in-law, Rona decided, but less handsome.

Then she chided herself for that thought. Peter Carlton was nothing to her.

He wasn't even Harlequin.

Was he?

The Earl spent some time admiring his daughter, then he smiled at Rona.

"Thank you," he said. "You both look exactly as I'd hoped."

"Isn't Miss Johnson pretty, Papa?"

"Very pretty," said the Earl, smiling at Rona warmly. "I shall be the proudest man at the table."

"Has the Russian Countess arrived?" Alice asked eagerly.

"Alice, that's enough," said Rona sharply. "A well-bred lady doesn't notice such things."

"What things?" the Earl wanted to know.

"I'm sorry, my Lord, but Alice is taking a most impertinent interest in Mr. Carlton and this Russian lady. I'm trying to make her realise that it is not at all 'the thing' to comment on other people in such a way."

"That's quite true," said the Earl, giving his daughter a wry look. "Still, I suppose it is fascinating. She's certainly very dashing, and Peter was at great pains to have her invited."

Alice threw Rona a triumphant look. "Is he madly in love with her, Papa?"

"I don't know about madly," said the Earl, "but he's certainly paying her a lot of attention. Shall we go, ladies?"

He offered them an arm each and they went out.

Rona knew she was looking her best in a gown of honey coloured silk trimmed with gold lace. Around her neck she wore a gilt chain, with a cameo.

As she descended the stairs several men in the hall looked up at her with admiration. Some of them pushed forward to meet her, and she wondered if she looked too fine for the position she was supposed to hold.

One man, though, did not even seem to notice her. Peter was deep in conversation with a black-haired woman who possessed a lush, startling beauty. Her mouth was full and ripe, and her eyes were so dark that it seemed as if they too were black.

She was making great play with her fan, but through the swishing movements Rona could see that Peter was holding her hand. She was looking up into his face (simpering, Rona thought in disgust), giving him the full power of her huge dark eyes. And he seemed entranced.

Monsieur Thierre greeted her with compliments about her own appearance and Alice's, and introduced his many offspring. First came Henri who was in his late twenties, then Marcel, a year younger. Two daughters, Marie and Agnes followed, then two more sons, Edouard and Jacques, and finally Cecile and Henriette, two girls of about Alice's age.

Jacques, a quiet, shy youth, was immediately taken with Alice, while Marcel and Henri were inclined to pay attention to Rona herself.

"And may I introduce some of my other guests?" said

Monsieur Thierre. "Countess Emilia Rostoya, currently visiting Paris from St. Petersburg."

Now Rona saw the Countess at close quarters she could better study her flamboyant beauty. Her mouth was very wide, and her brilliant smiles showed gleaming white teeth.

To Rona there was something cruel about those smiles. It was as if the Countess was confident of her power to enslave any man.

There was no doubt about it. This woman was an adventuress.

There was a man with her, Count Alexei Rostoy, who turned out to be her brother. He was a big man with broad shoulders, black hair and a huge swirling moustache of the same colour. In fact, it was such a startling jet black that Rona could not help wondering if he had dyed it.

She found herself sitting next to him at dinner. To her relief he spoke good English, and seemed pleasant, if not very bright.

"That Peter, he's a devil," the Count said cheerfully. "He hadn't been in Paris for ten minutes before he was chasing my sister."

"Indeed?" Rona said politely.

"It wouldn't surprise me if he came here to find her."

"Do you live in Paris all the time?"

"Oh no! Emilia and I like to travel around. We are very cosmopolitan. Unfortunately we have expensive tastes, so I am looking for an heiress. Do you know any heiresses?"

Coming after Lord Robert's deviousness this frank approach was almost charming. Rona gave an involuntary little choke of laughter.

"You find me amusing?" asked the Count. "That is most distressing. I assure you, my dear young lady, that money is a most serious business."

"I agree," she said firmly.

"You see, in my own way, I am an honest man. You are a most beautiful woman. But, since you are earning your living, it follows that you have no money. Therefore I must say to you that while I might adore and worship you and while I might think you a goddess that no man could possibly resist – marriage between us is impossible."

She turned glassy eyes on him.

"I beg your pardon?"

"I sympathise with your disappointment, but is it not better for me to be frank?"

Rona's lips twitched. She was beginning to like him.

"I can't say I wasn't warned, can I?" she said.

"That is my object."

"So I would suppose. I would imagine, sir, that your life has been full of ladies complaining that they weren't warned in time."

"You are right," he said gravely. "It is better to be safe."

Their eyes met. At the same moment they both went into gales of laughter. Everyone at the table stopped to turn and look at them, smiling.

Monsieur Thierre was delighted to see his guests mixing so well, but Rona quickly checked herself, fearing lest the Earl should think she was setting his daughter an example of unladylike behaviour.

But the Earl only smiled at her quizzically. Peter, facing her across the table, also had a quizzical look on his face, but he wasn't smiling, and there was a darkness in his eyes. Then the Countess tapped his arm and he immediately returned his attention to her. After that he seemed oblivious to anything Rona said or did.

"Beautiful lady," said Count Rostoy fervently.

"That's enough," said Rona. "You are drawing people's attention to me, and I do not like it."

"You are right. It is better to wait until we are alone."

Receiving no answer, he sighed.

"Alas, I bore you already."

Rona barely heard him. Her attention had been drawn by Alice, sitting next to Jacques, the youngest son. He seemed totally smitten with her, and she was flowering under his attention. She was also, Rona noted, learning a lot of new French words.

Her eyes met the Earl's across the table. She glanced significantly at Alice and smiled. He nodded, understanding her perfectly, and returned her smile.

Rona turned back to the Count.

"I do wish you would tell me about Russia," she said sincerely. "It's a country that has always fascinated me."

He began to do so, describing the court of Czar Alexander II, which he seemed to know well, although not, she suspected, as well as he claimed. He talked about the jewels and the splendid clothes, and the great ceremonies in the cathedral.

But he also talked about his home in the country, where the landscape stretched to a far horizon, seemingly endless. He talked about spring and silver birch trees and songs floating on the air as the peasants walked home from the fields.

Rona listened entranced, liking him more and more. She was in no danger of falling in love with this cheerful, overgrown child, but he was agreeable company.

When dinner was over, the party adjourned to the music room. Various guests took it in turns to strum on the piano, while the others mingled, murmuring softly.

"I've never seen Alice come out of her shell like this," the Earl said to Rona. "But are you sure she's not coming out too fast."

"She's safe enough while we both keep an eye on her," Rona said. "That boy is little more than a child himself. It's a game to both of them. And I think Alice has suffered from too little praise and attention. A little of too much won't harm her."

"You're right. I leave it in your hands," he said warmly. "For I never knew anyone I trusted more."

He enclosed her hand in both of his for a moment, then turned away to talk to his hostess.

Count Rostoy immediately commandeered Rona's attention again.

"Are you sure you're wise to spend so much time with me?" she asked. "You might be overlooking an heiress."

"You are very kind to think of my problems, but concern is needless," he said gravely. "Monsieur Thierre's daughters are either married or too young. The little Alice is also too young. If I tried to be gallant, her Papa would slit my throat."

"Or I might do it for him," Rona agreed cheerfully.

"Exactly, so you see, there are no possibilities here. I have checked carefully."

"Of course. I should have known that you would not overlook such a detail," she returned with equal gravity. But her eyes were dancing.

Again they laughed together, but quietly this time, not to attract too much attention.

He continued talking about Moscow and St. Petersburg, and she listened in delight, until one young woman, anxious to display her skill at the piano embarked on a piece that was very long and very loud.

"Let us slip onto the terrace," said the Count. "We can talk more quietly there."

They did so, moving out of range of the pianist, but staying within sight, for the sake of delicacy, so that anyone who was interested could look out and see the good looking man and woman, laughing with their heads together, happily engrossed in each other's company.

They stayed like that for an hour, until Rona recollected herself and declared that it was time for Alice to go to bed.

*

At breakfast, the next morning, Marcel said,

"Ladies, would it suit you to ride in the Bois de Boulogne this morning?"

"We would be glad to escort you," added young Jacques, with a sigh in Alice's direction.

Neither Rona nor Alice had riding habits with them, but the ladies of the family were generous in lending theirs, which were new and in the very latest style.

"I look so grown up," Alice said, thrilled.

"Well remember you are not quite seventeen," Rona warned her. "Try to behave sedately."

Alice made a face.

Rona tried not to be vain about her own appearance, but the riding habit showed off her trim figure to advantage. Outside the sun was shining.

The Earl and Monsieur Thierre had gone out together to attend some conference. Peter was also missing, and Marcel mentioned that he had left early that morning, 'on urgent business'. Thus a party of eight set off for the Bois de Boulogne.

Jacques had easily manoeuvred himself so that he was riding next to Alice, and there was a certain amount of jostling to get beside Rona. It was Marcel who prevailed. He played practised court to her, admiring her looks and her riding, until eventually she laughed.

"Have I offended you, that you laugh at me?" he asked.

"No, I'm not offended. I'm just enjoying the novelty of compliments. In England they're in very short supply. That's what's so nice about coming here, because you always say such charming things, even if you don't mean them."

"Of course we mean them when it concerns anyone as pretty as you," Marcel replied promptly.

Rona laughed again.

"Now that's the sort of compliment I like," she said, "and which I wouldn't get in my country."

Marcel nodded.

"I've been to England, and I think the reason the Englishmen are very mean with their compliments is simply because they don't know how to enjoy themselves, especially when it concerns pretty women.

"And the trouble with English women is that they are so unused to compliments that they cannot believe them."

"I promise to believe every word you say," Rona laughed.

"Good. And when you return home, you must give the Englishmen a lesson in how to behave towards women. Tell them we manage better over here."

"I'll try but I don't think all the lessons in the world will make an Englishman as skilled as a Frenchman."

They continued bantering in this cheerful way until they were deep into the park. Then suddenly Rona heard a new voice beside her.

"My compliments ma'am. After a wearying journey and a late night you still manage to be as fresh as a daisy this morning."

Turning her head quickly she was startled to see Peter, astride a jet black horse and looking magnificent.

"I did not think you meant to join us, sir," she said. "You are supposed to be elsewhere."

"Oh, I manage to be everywhere," he said lightly.

And suddenly she heard another voice, in another place, saying,

"Harlequin is everywhere, and sees everything."

A tremor went through her. It was him. Now she was sure it was him. Hearing words so similar she recognised the tone in the voice.

She twisted in the saddle to regard him intently.

He was looking at her, and there was something in his eyes that might have been recognition.

She waited for him to confirm her suspicions.

"Your charge is a credit to you," he said at last. "I have seldom seen her in such good spirits."

Good manners forced her to conceal her disappointment.

"I can take little credit for that, sir. I've been in the Earl's employment only two days."

"I think you can take every credit. It's not a question of time, but of attitude. When we met, Alice told me you were magic, because that's how you made her feel. She was unhappy, and you made her happy. That's true magic."

"Thank you," she said, taken aback.

They rode a little further and then he said,

"I was very fond of my sister, Valerie. We grew close after our parents died. When she married and had a child, they became my family too. Giles has always encouraged me to treat his house as my own, and now I feel almost like a second father to Alice. I'm grateful to you for what you've done for her."

"The poor child needs a woman's guidance now she's growing up," said Rona. "With her father being an Earl, so many men are going to approach her for the wrong reasons."

"You mean fortune hunters?"

"I am afraid so. She must learn to recognise them."

"But you can teach her that better than anyone."

"Why do you say so?" she asked quickly.

Now he was going to tell her that they had met before.

"Because, ma'am, you seem to be pursuing a secret vendetta against men." He spoke lightly, and with a sideways smile at her.

"I'm doing no such thing," Rona retorted.

"You clearly disapprove of us all – except perhaps those with big black moustaches. I wonder why."

She maintained a diplomatic silence. She had the feeling that he was deliberately fencing with her.

"We're not all rogues," he pleaded.

"Indeed?"

"You can't be so hard hearted as to believe that."

"I can believe whatever I think I have reason for," she said with a little toss of her head.

"I see what it is. Some shabby fellow let you down and broke your heart. Tell me the scoundrel's name and I'll run him through."

"Certainly not. And my heart is far from broken. In fact, it's firmly in my own possession and always has been."

"Ah! A lady of taste and discernment. I like that."

"You are impertinent, sir. I have no interest in what you like."

"Foiled again!" he said with an exaggerated sigh that made her laugh. "Well, I guessed that winning your good opinion wasn't going to be easy."

"Probably quite impossible," she said.

"Would it help if I grew a moustache?" he asked hopefully.

"You haven't the style for it. I advise you not to waste your time."

"But I never take good advice, ma'am. It's the code I live by."

"Then you will surely come to grief."

After a moment he said in a strange voice,

"How do you know I haven't already come to grief?"

She hesitated, not sure how to reply. He could have meant so many things.

"Well, if you have, you're very cheerful under it," she said, trying to gain time.

"But how do you know that what you see is real?" he asked. "Perhaps I'm really wearing a mask?"

Her heart began to beat quickly.

"I think you would wear a mask better than most people," she agreed. "Perhaps several."

He gave a quick intake of breath as though her words had gone home. She was startled by the sight of his face which had grown suddenly pale.

"Astute of you, ma'am," he said in a soft voice. "A shrewd guess? Or are you too, perhaps, wearing a mask?"

"Do you believe I am?"

He had recovered himself and was looking at her, with a curious half smile. She noticed again what a wide, mobile mouth he had, and suddenly she was assailed by the memory of firm lips covering her own, moving seductively in a kiss given by a man determined that she should never forget him.

'Was it you?' she thought desperately. 'Was it your arms that held me, your mouth that caressed mine until I could not think, only feel?'

In a moment surely he would say something to end her confusion.

Then she heard a shout from behind. Somebody said, "Hey, look who's over there."

Everybody's eyes turned to where the Countess Rostoya and her brother were cantering towards them.

"I must pay my respects," said Peter. "Your pardon ma'am."

He tipped his hat to Rona and, with no further ado, spurred his horse forward towards the Countess. Rona saw him pull up beside her, take her hand in his and kiss it fervently.

The spell was broken. One moment she had held all his attention, and he had seemed on the verge of saying something momentous.

But now he had forgotten all about her.

CHAPTER SIX

By common consent the two parties joined up. Count Rostoy immediately fell in beside Rona, seized her hand, kissed it and pressed it theatrically to his bosom. Since his behaviour reminded her more of clowning than of passion, she was not offended.

"I have spent the whole night thinking of your beauty," he said in throbbing accents.

"What a shocking waste of time!" she declared. "You should have been thinking of heiresses."

"True, but what can I do when you are so beautiful and so cruel?"

From behind them came the sound of a giggle. Alice was listening and enjoying herself. Not in the least disconcerted, the Count turned and saluted her, grinning.

The Russian didn't have everything as he pleased. Henri, determined not to be outdone by his brother, Marcel, joined Rona on the other side and made a determined bid for her attention. He and the Count enjoyed a cheerful duel for the next mile, but they were both baulked by the fact that the lady's attention kept wandering. She was trying to keep Alice in view.

Sometimes this was easy as the girl rode almost level with her. Sometimes she fell behind, and sometimes she began to drift off down side paths, with the two younger sons, and Rona had to call her back. Alice would make a face, but she always returned obediently.

It pleased Rona to see that Alice was a very good rider. Her horse was docile, and presented little challenge, but the girl clearly had a natural skill.

Rona's own mount was more spirited and she had to concentrate to keep it under control. But her Papa had insisted on her being taught by the best teachers, and she emerged the winner from their battle of wills.

Henri, who owned the animal, congratulated her.

"Castor is lively, but you have the trick of making him obey you."

"Thank you," she said lightly, "but that shouldn't surprise you. A governess has to know the art of commanding obedience, with horses as in everything."

"Ah yes! In everything! I think, Mademoiselle Governess, that this describes you. You are – now, what is the English word?"

"Bossy," Rona informed him merrily.

"Ah yes! Bossy!"

"But this is an insult," roared the Russian. "A woman doesn't like to be called bossy."

"That depends how bossy she actually is," Rona pointed out. Meeting Henri's eye with a teasing glance, she added, "she might be glad of it, as a way of signalling the slavish obedience that she expects."

"You see?" Henri declared triumphantly.

"Well it seems a strange sort of flirting to me," the Count grumbled.

"But sometimes," Henri took up her theme, "a man is too obstinate to listen to her. Actually, if we are honest, from the day of his marriage he is struggling to be the head of the house, and not just an obedient man of no distinction in it."

Rona laughed.

"I am sure that will never happen to you," she said.

"I wish I were as certain. I'm afraid, in case I fail, and find myself trampled on by pretty feminine feet."

"A woman has to be very strong to fight a man," Rona mused. "The best thing is to entice him, so that it's too late before he realises what is happening."

Henri grinned.

"You are incorrigible," he said, "and I am really sorry for your husband when you marry, as I'm quite certain you will always get your own way."

"I'll fight for it," Rona observed, "if I think I'm right – "

"But a lady always thinks she's in the right," said Peter's voice.

Somehow he had slipped in behind her, and listened to the conversation.

"I don't admit that for moment," she retorted. "However I'm always ready to bow to any man whose ideas are better than mine."

"Aha! And there's the catch," said Peter. "Who decides whose ideas are better? Why, the lady, of course."

"And that's how it should be," Rona declared, to general laughter.

Then something happened that took everyone's attention from their merry party. Behind them there were shouts of anger and dismay, galloping hooves, followed by the sound of gunshots. Everyone looked around to see a group of very young men on horseback, tearing down the path at speed, firing pistols into the air as they went.

Henri made a sound of disgust.

"They are racing, which is forbidden here. Also they seem to be drunk."

"In that case, they're probably Englishmen," Peter observed wryly, moving his horse so that he could shield Countess Emilia.

"I'm sure one of them is Russian," Count Rostoy said, gallantly willing to share the blame. "But whatever they are, it's disgraceful before ladies."

"You're right," said Henri. "Let us take the ladies aside."

But before they could move the horsemen were upon them, firing madly into the air, and making a commotion that unsettled the animals. Everyone looked to their mounts, and quietened them, but the horse that became most agitated was Rona's.

A particularly loud shot made Castor rear so that she had to fight to keep her seat. The next moment he had bolted.

She had known he was spirited, but as he thundered away she discovered that he was far too strong for her. She fought grimly to hang on, but he resisted all her efforts to control him, or even to guide his direction.

People fled from her path. She had no idea where she was going, or what was going to happen. She could only cling on and pray.

She was vaguely aware of two other horses being hard driven and coming up beside her, one each side. She thought the rider on the left was Peter, but she dared not look. It was taking all her skill and concentration to avoid being thrown.

Then she saw a stretch of water just ahead. She pulled on Castor's head, but he kept pounding on. A man's hand reached out for the bridle, trying to turn her away from the water, but at the very last moment Castor swerved sharply to the left, crossing Peter's horse and causing it to rear violently.

A woman screamed. Something struck Rona. The

next moment she was flying over Castor's head into the water. It broke her fall slightly, but she still landed hard enough to be stunned.

For a moment she flailed, gasping for breath, terrified of sinking and drowning. Then a pair of strong arms hauled her to the surface and up out of the water, lifting her high against a broad chest.

Her head swam.

Peter, she thought. Peter had saved her.

Blindly she reached up one arm and put it about his neck.

Then a loud but kindly voice said,

"That's it. You are safe now. Hold on to me."

It was Count Alexei.

He was striding back through the water to where their party had gathered in a crowd on the bank. There were murmurs of concern and dismay.

"We must take her home at once," said Henri. "Can she ride, or should I send home for a carriage?"

"That would take too long," said the Count. "She will ride with me. See?"

Before she knew it the Count had climbed back into this saddle and taken her up before him.

"I – I'm all right," she said, dazed. "I can ride – "

"I think not," he said. "You would fall if you tried to ride alone."

If only, she thought, it had been Peter who held her in his arms on the journey home. As it was, she could have cried from mortification that such a thing should have happened.

Images swirled about her. There was Peter's face, white and tense, but he was keeping back, beside the Countess. And there was Alice, tearful and distraught.

"Miss Johnson," she cried. "Oh, please don't be dead."

"Don't be a silly girl," Rona rallied her in as strong a voice as she could manage. "Of course I'm not dead. It was just a little tumble."

The world seemed to swim as she spoke and she was forced to cling on to the Count. He urged his horse on and in a few moments they had left the park.

How terribly her head ached where it had been struck. She had only a vague impression of the journey home and then there was Madame Thierre full of horror at her guest's plight.

She was conveyed upstairs and a doctor hurriedly summoned. He declared that the blow on her head was not serious and a long sleep would see her well again. Madame Thierre brought up a cordial, and hovered anxiously by the bed.

"I'm so sorry to be a nuisance," Rona said, feeling despondent.

"But of course you are not," said her hostess. "It was an accident."

"I should have been looking after Alice."

"Alice is well, and asking to see you."

Alice had brought a surprise with her.

"My Lord," exclaimed Rona, struggling up in bed, aghast at the sight of the Earl. "Oh, they shouldn't have troubled you."

"Of course they sent for me," said the Earl, very pale. "I would have been very annoyed not to have been informed."

"I've let you down."

"Nonsense," he said kindly, sitting on the bed and taking her hand between his. "You're not to worry about anything. Peter and I will look after Alice. Peter sent you his apologies, by the way. Apparently it was his horse that kicked you in the head."

"So that was it," Rona murmured. "It was my fault really. I cut across him and the horse reared."

"So I gathered from that Russian Countess, when she could make sense of anything. She became hysterical and had to be calmed with promises of an expensive gift. Peter has taken her off to a jeweller's shop."

"I see," she said in a colourless voice.

"Yes, nobody really likes her," said the Earl, misunderstanding her tone. "Everyone was grateful when he removed her, even if it is going to cost him more than he can afford."

"Perhaps he can afford more than anybody knows," Rona said lightly.

"I shouldn't think so, unless he's picked up a fortune on his numerous travels. And she won't bring him any money. He must be deeply in love to follow her as he does."

"Really."

"I'm tiring you. I'll go now. But be careful in future. I wish I could join you all when you go riding, then I could keep a friendly eye on you."

"Why don't you try?" said Rona at once. "Alice would love that."

"It's hard for me to take time off. Monsieur Thierre is making it possible for me to meet many people in the financial world, and I have to give that most of my attention.

"Besides," he added after a thoughtful moment, "perhaps I would be in the way?"

"Of course not. How can you think that?"

He didn't look at her as he said,

"From what I hear, you might be about to announce

your engagement to our Russian friend."

"Oh no," she said at once. "He's looking for an heiress, so he can't afford to marry a poor girl like me. He told me so straight away."

"He actually said that?" the Earl demanded, aghast. "The fellow's a bounder."

"Not at all. Just honest. He makes me laugh, my Lord. That's why I enjoy his company."

"Good heavens!" exclaimed the Earl, startled. "Better keep him away from Alice, though."

"No, he knows that if he flirted with her you'd put an end to him. And if you didn't, I would. I told him that."

He gave her a wry look.

"I shall never understand ladies. You must be very strong minded to talk in such a way."

"Some people would say frivolous."

"They're wrong," he said firmly. "I like to be cheered up."

She felt warmed. He was such a nice man, not inspiring or thrilling, but with a resolute kindness and decency.

He left her and she drifted off into sleep. But even there her thoughts were troubled.

It was time to be sensible.

Peter was not Harlequin, whatever lingering echoes might haunt her. It was impossible, because her heart told her that Harlequin would not have abandoned her for another woman.

Nothing had really changed.

And yet she had the strangest feeling of having lost something.

The doctor's medicine made her sleep well and when

she woke it was morning. She felt refreshed and stronger and insisted on getting up, despite Alice's protests.

"But the bruise on your forehead!" the girl exclaimed.

"It looks worse than it is. I'm hungry. A good, hearty breakfast and I'll be ready for anything."

This proved to be an exaggeration. There was consternation when she appeared downstairs, but her hosts agreed that food would be good for her.

Her place at table was a mass of flowers. Everybody wanted to spoil her. One of the daughters made her a present of some embroidered handkerchiefs. In her weakened state she was almost in tears at the affection and generosity.

But when breakfast was over, her strength seemed to fade again and she knew she needed to rest some more.

In the end Madame Thierre arranged for a reclining chair to be carried out under the trees, and Rona was settled against cushions and told to relax and think only of getting better.

Alice was full of sweet concern, running back several times with extra cushions, asking if she wanted anything else.

"All I need is to know that you're going to be all right," Rona said.

"Madame Thierre is taking me to see some shops with her daughters. Uncle Peter said he would take me out later, but this morning he's gone to see the Countess." She made a face. "Once he's with her he'll probably forget all about me."

"I'm sure he won't," Rona assured her.

"I'm sure he will. Papa says he's never seen a man so in love."

At last she left and Rona could have peace. She felt depressed and weary, and all she wanted to do was close her eyes and let the world drift away.

She did not know how long she slept, but suddenly she was awake, and very much aware, although her eyes were still closed. When she opened them she received a shock.

Peter was standing there, his eyes fixed on her, his tense face very pale.

"What are you doing out here?" he demanded sharply. "You should be in bed."

"I'll go back upstairs soon, but the sun is lovely."

"You shouldn't take risks with an injury to the head," he told her, still in the same rough tone.

"It's only a little bump."

"Nonsense, you don't know what you're talking about," he snapped.

She stared in surprise at his rude tone, but he strode away at once, not meeting her eyes. After walking a few steps he halted and looked back. She thought he was about to say something, but he only took a deep breath and turned away again.

Then he stopped once more and came back to where she was reclining.

"Are you angry with me?" Rona asked. "Was your horse injured?"

"To blazes with the horse!" he snapped. "Do you think I'm worried about a horse?"

"Then I don't know why you're so angry."

To her amazement he muttered something under his breath that might even have been a curse. Rona had not seen him so agitated. He seemed to be under the influence of some torturing emotion that he could neither voice nor control.

"I'm not angry," he said at last. "I just want to put you on your guard."

"About what?"

He took a sharp breath.

"Count Rostoy. The way you allow him to behave towards you is – is – " He swung away again.

Rona pulled herself up from her reclining position, scarcely able to believe her ears.

"Is what?" she demanded indignantly.

"Unsuitable!" he said at last.

"And exactly what do you mean by that?"

"I mean that his manners are too unrestrained."

This was intolerable. After flaunting his devotion to Countess Emilia before her eyes, he dared question her friendship with Emilia's brother.

In her anger she got to her feet and faced him.

"I have no fault to find with the Count's manners," she said stiffly.

He glared.

"I repeat, they are inappropriate. It amazes me that you haven't seen it yourself. Or are you so enamoured of him that he is allowed to make free with your hand in public, something to which you clearly do not object."

"Of course I don't. It was only a joke. I'd have had to be a great ninny to make a scene about something so silly. Are you daring to say that my behaviour has been improper?"

"I say that it has been incautious, especially remembering that a young girl is in your charge. Did Alice appreciate the 'joke'?"

"More than anyone. In fact it was a very valuable lesson for her – how to react when a man makes a fool of himself." Her eyes flashed as she added, "something which she will encounter with depressing regularity during her life. Every woman does. I only wish she could be here to witness this scene. She'd learn even more about male foolishness than she did yesterday morning."

She had the satisfaction of seeing him lost for words, and continued the attack.

"May I remind you that Count Rostoy rescued me? And – " now she came to her real grievance, " – he was the only one who did."

"On the contrary, I did my best to assist you, and would have done so if you hadn't alarmed my horse," Peter replied.

"A horse over which you appeared to have no control." She knew this was deeply unfair, but that was nothing beside the pleasure of infuriating him. "Whatever you meant to do, Count Rostoy was the man who actually saved me. Shall I snub him after that? Pretty behaviour indeed!"

"Very well, madam," he snapped. "You have made your partiality clear beyond misunderstanding. I didn't think you could be misled by a loud voice and a raucous manner. I estimated you as a woman of character. I blame myself for the mistake."

She stared at him, almost gaping.

How could she ever have mistaken this man for a gentleman? To speak to a woman in such a way! And a sick woman at that!

It was beside the point that, at this precise moment, she did not feel ill. On the contrary. She felt possessed by a glorious fury that filled her with new strength. It was a positive pleasure to give as good as she got.

"I repeat," she said emphatically, "that I have no fault to find with his manners. I have, however, much fault to find with yours. I am accountable to Lord Lancing, not to you. If he has no complaint to make of me, then you should have none."

His eyes gleamed. "Have I not?"

"No sir, you have not. If you object to my behaviour, I suggest you approach my employer. If he is displeased, he can dismiss me."

"Of course I don't want to see you dismissed," he said raggedly. "But you allow Count Rostoy intimacies which – that is, he is not an acceptable person for you to know."

"And his sister?" she flashed.

The words were unladylike, but she could not help herself, and she had the satisfaction of knowing that they had gone home. His expression tightened, and his eyes flashed anger.

"We will leave her out of this discussion, if you please," he said coldly.

"Certainly. Let us leave them both out of this discussion. Kindly understand, once and for all, that my friendships do not concern you."

"The devil they – " he began angrily. Then he stopped and his face changed. Anger left from it, to be replaced by fear. "What is it? What's the matter?"

Her feeling of well-being had suddenly drained away, leaving her faint and exhausted from the very strength of her anger. The world swam about her. Through the mists she saw his face, pale and distraught, felt his hands seize her, heard his cry of "Rona! *My God, Rona!*"

Then she felt herself lifted in his arms. He was running to the house and up the stairs, crying, "Get the doctor!"

She was being carried upstairs, clasped in his arms, and it felt so different to being carried by the Count. It felt so safe, so wonderful.

He kicked open her bedroom door. Then he laid her on her bed and retreated, leaving her in the hands of the women who hurried in. Her last view was of his face, the mask stripped away, his eyes wild and horrified.

The doctor arrived again and reproved her for getting up too soon.

"But I was lying down," she protested. "Most of the time, anyway. It's just that I was outside instead of in bed."

"And how did you get so agitated that you collapsed?" he asked wryly. "Perhaps you were watching the thrilling antics of a bird?"

"No, of course not."

"Or maybe you had a quarrel with your lover?" he asked, his eyes twinkling.

"He is not my lover," she said, so emphatically that the well-meaning little man retired discomfited.

She had supper in bed. Alice brought it in and fussed over her like a mother hen.

"Have you got everything you need?" she asked for the hundredth time.

"Yes," Rona laughed. She was feeling well again. "You're going to kill me with kindness."

"Oh, I nearly forgot, Uncle Peter asked me to give you this."

She showed Rona a little box, wrapped in gold paper.

"Another present," she said. "Isn't that nice of him? Mind you," she added with an air of worldly wisdom, "I expect the Countess helped him choose it."

Rona was unwrapping the paper and opening the box inside. At last Peter's gift of a small china figurine lay in her hand.

"No," she said softly. "I don't think anyone else chose this."

It was a Harlequin.

CHAPTER SEVEN

The next day Rona waited to see Peter, to ask him about the figurine. Surely, now he would admit to being Harlequin? And then there were so many questions she wanted to ask him.

But he did not come to see her.

At Madame Thierre's insistence she remained in bed another two days. During that time she was bombarded with red roses from Alexei.

"My own offering looks quite trivial beside them," Lord Lancing said, extending his hand, bearing a small bouquet of white roses, and smiling ruefully.

"I prefer these," Rona said, taking the roses. "Thank you. Perhaps somebody could take those ridiculous red ones away."

"Poor Count Rostoy. How his heart would grieve at your rejection of his offering!"

"Count Rostoy enjoys making theatrical gestures, but he has no more a heart for me than I have for him," Rona said firmly. "He makes me laugh, and that's the best I can say of him."

"Except that he saved your life," the Earl reminded her.

"I suppose so. But the water was only three feet deep, and if he hadn't waded in someone else would have done."

The Earl roared with laughter.

"How appallingly practical women are!"

"I just don't see Count Rostoy as a hero."

"I'm glad of that," he said simply.

On the second day she came down for dinner, to the acclaim of the whole family.

The Earl led her downstairs, her arm in his, and there were more little gifts by her plate. Peter smiled as if nothing untoward had happened between them.

For once the Count and Countess were not there, which Rona found a relief. She would not have to sit and watch Peter flirting outrageously with the beautiful Russian, and they could talk later.

The whole family seemed to have taken to her. They murmured approval as the Earl took her to sit beside him at the table, and watched in delight as she opened her gifts.

"That'll be you very soon," Peter told Alice, who was watching eagerly. "Unless I've got the dates wrong, you'll be seventeen next week."

"That's right," said Alice, smiling ecstatically.

"You'd better start thinking what you want for a present," said Peter, grinning back at her.

"There's only one present I want," said Alice. "To stay in Paris forever and ever. Oh Papa, can't we?"

"And what about our home in England?" the Earl reminded her wryly. "Surely you don't want to leave that 'forever and ever'?"

"No, we'll go back one day, but couldn't we stay for a while? Oh, please, Papa!"

"But why not?" asked Monsieur Thierre. "After such a long journey you must not go home too soon. You should at least stay long enough for Alice to spend her birthday here."

Everybody agreed that this was a good idea, especially Jacques and Edouard, who were almost at daggers drawn over Alice's charms. At last it was decided.

"What could I do but give in?" the Earl asked Rona a few moments later. "She wants to stay so much."

Rona smiled and agreed. But it had seemed to her that it was Peter who wanted to prolong their stay, and he had known just how to bring it about.

She decided to ask him about it after dinner.

But when the gentlemen joined the ladies there was no sign of Peter.

"He said he had business to attend to," said the Earl. "Which probably means a night's carousing."

"I thought Peter had virtually abandoned his old pursuits to pursue the Countess," quipped Monsieur Thierre in English.

Next to Alice young Cecile sighed. "I wish Papa wouldn't make jokes in English. He always checks afterwards to see if I understood, and then I get a lecture about working harder to learn English."

"My governesses used to lecture me about my French," said Alice sympathetically.

"Tables to learn by heart – " said Cecile at once.

"Verbs – "

"Adjectives – "

They regarded each other sympathetically.

Rona happened to be standing just behind them, and repeated the conversation to the Earl.

"Now they regard each other as sisters in suffering," she said, wryly. "And Alice realises that she isn't the only one."

"Am I imagining it, or is her French improving?"

"By leaps and bounds. Those two boys are her willing slaves, and it's doing more for her than all the lessons in the world. Poor lads."

"Why do you say that?"

"Because they're seventeen and eighteen. Next week's birthday will transform Alice."

"Ah yes, they'll look like children to her, won't they? And soon she'll be officially a debutante." He grinned. "As you say, poor lads."

"I want to talk to you about Alice," said Madame Thierre, appearing with coffee. "We would like to mark her birthday by giving a ball for her here."

"That's kind of you but there's no need, madame," said the Earl quickly. "After all, you were rather backed into a corner by my daughter."

"Not by her," Madame Thierre laughed. "It was Peter who wanted an excuse to stay in Paris and continue courting the lovely Emilia. I think it's so delightful, and we are happy to help him. Perhaps at the ball they'll make an announcement."

"It's about time he settled down and gave up his rackety way of life," the Earl agreed. "Not that Emilia is really a 'settling down' kind of woman. Clearly he's madly in love with her, and she'll lead him a merry dance."

Madame Thierre nodded.

"Between you and me I don't think he's gone carousing tonight at all – unless it's with Emilia."

They laughed together comfortably.

Rona turned away so that they couldn't see her face. Out of sight she was grinding her nails into her palms.

After that she could take no further pleasure in the evening.

If only he would return and she could speak to him.

Then, perhaps, her heart could be at ease.

She began to wish the night away and the morning to come.

But next day he had disappeared.

*

"He is a most extraordinary young man," Madame Thierre told the others over breakfast, "I came downstairs early this morning to find Peter waiting for me. He bade me a charming farewell and positively begged my forgiveness. Of course I told him no forgiveness was necessary and he could return whenever he pleased, as long as it's in time for Alice's ball."

"But will he?" asked Cecile.

Madame Thierre shrugged. "Who can say? We've known him for several years, and if there's one thing I've learned it's that you never know where and when he's going to appear next."

The Earl nodded. "My wife used to say he was like a Jack-In-The-Box," he said. "He was always where you least expected, vanishing without warning and returning in the nick of time.

"Take last week. He arrives in London, comes straight to my house only just in time to join us on this trip. A few hours later and he'd have missed us."

Hearing him say that, Rona had a strange feeling. She was sure now that Peter was Harlequin, which meant that he had been in London for at least a day longer than his brother-in-law believed, since he had been at the Westminster ball.

Why should Peter have lied about such a thing?

And she remembered again how he had vanished when his friends tried to greet him at the ball. Like a man who was hiding something.

One moment he behaved as though he were drawn to

her, just as she was to him. The next, he fled from her. Why had he acted like that in the garden, almost as though he hated her, only to send her a gift that she alone would understand? If she meant something to him, why did he behave like a moth to the Countess's flame, oblivious of any other woman?

Why had he suddenly disappeared, just when she wanted to confront him with the Harlequin figurine?

Or was that the reason?

"He'll turn up when he turns up," said the Earl. "He has lots of friends in France. He probably wanted to make sure he visited them all before we leave."

He eyed his daughter mischievously.

"Now, about this ball. You understand that I can't afford to spend any money on your gown. I'm sure Miss Johnson can find you something suitable in the clothes you have."

"*Papa!*" Alice almost screamed.

"Don't be a silly girl," Rona chided her. "Your Papa doesn't mean that. He's going to buy you a new pair of gloves."

Aghast, Alice looked from one to the other, while the rest of the family rocked with laughter.

"Of course you must have a new dress," said Madame Thierre. "Several new dresses, in fact. We shall go immediately to the Rue de la Paix, and stay there as long as necessary."

The gentlemen immediately thought of other things they needed to do, and in a short while the ladies were on their way.

Before he departed the Earl had spoken quietly to Rona, instructing her to spare no expense in fitting out his daughter.

"But don't tell her I said so," he warned, with a twinkle in his eyes, "or she'll be quite impossible."

"Don't worry," Rona agreed.

"Also, there is the question of your own attire," he said, seeming to become uneasy. "I know you're not an ordinary governess and you seem able to afford better clothes than most of them. Just the same, a ball given by the Thierres is going to be a very grand occasion, and you should be dressed like the other ladies. That being the case – " he seemed about to expire from embarrassment, "I think the purchase of your gown should be my responsibility."

"You are very kind, my Lord, but that cannot be," Rona said firmly.

"Please don't misunderstand me," he said awkwardly. "I didn't mean – what you think I meant."

Rona understood. A lady did not allow a gentleman to dress her unless she also allowed him to undress her. That was why no lady ever accepted an item of wearing apparel from a man. The only exception was between engaged couples, and even then it must be no more than a scarf or a handkerchief.

The Earl's idea was, therefore, outrageous, although she acquitted him of dishonourable intent. His miserable confusion testified to his honesty.

But she had no doubt what her answer must be.

"I'm sorry, my Lord, but what you suggest is impossible. I do have some decent clothes, and I trust I shall not shame you at the ball. If I dress less lavishly than everyone else, that is only proper. I am, after all, still a governess. Nobody will think it strange. Please, do not be offended at my refusal."

"I'm not offended," he said quietly. "I honour you for your strength of mind. You are a true lady."

His words stayed with her on the journey to the Rue de la Paix, along with a certain gentleness in his manner. But all brooding ceased when they reached their destination and she found herself surrounded by a riot of silks, satins, brocades and gauzes.

First Madame Thierre had to speak to the head of the establishment, a tiny woman with bright eyes, called Ginette. Then the two of them exclaimed over Alice, her youth, her beauty, her dainty figure. Agnes and Cecile joined in, walking round Alice, discussing her points as they would have done a horse.

Alice had no objection. She was filled with bliss to be the centre of attention for such a delightful reason, and could gladly have stood there all day while the rival merits of various fabrics were debated.

In the end they decided on white silk gauze. Ginette took Alice's measurements and produced some styles. Pouring over these took the rest of the day. By the time they returned home everybody was in the last stages of exhaustion. The men thought this was very funny and teased them over dinner.

The following day they returned to Ginette's establishment. As they were climbing down from the carriage Alexei walked past, and saluted them with a flourish. Rona stopped to speak to him, thinking that he might mention Peter, if she appeared only casually interested.

But when she mentioned that Peter had gone, Alexei looked surprised and said,

"Him too? Everyone is vanishing from Paris. Emilia is away for a while visiting friends and I am all alone."

Madame Thierre immediately invited him for the evening. Rona tried to look pleased although she felt, after what she had just heard, that nothing could ever please her again.

At the end of five days everyone, except Rona, had new gowns, shoes, scarves, gloves. Jewellery was brought out from safes and polished. There was to be one more visit to Ginette, and then all was done.

It was a merry occasion. Alice put on her completed dress and went out into the corridor to parade up and down before the mirrors that lined one wall, looking at herself this way and that, studying the dress from all angles, while everyone cried approval.

Then they crowded back into the dressing room. Ginette produced a bottle of champagne, and even the young girls were allowed a sip.

As she was enjoying her glass of champagne, Rona heard a sound from the corridor that alerted her.

It was a woman's laugh, rich, vibrant, sensual. It told the world that this was a woman with a lover, or perhaps many lovers, and she was confident in her power to captivate them all.

It was Emilia.

So the Russian woman had returned from wherever she had been.

Moving slowly, so as not to attract attention, Rona slid out into the corridor. As she had expected, Countess Emilia Rostoya was stalking up and down, studying herself in detail in the huge mirrors.

Her dress was deep crimson velvet. For all her voluptuous build Emilia had the tiny waist of a young girl, which served to emphasise the size and magnificence of her bosom. It was further emphasised by the fact that the dress plunged low in the front (indecently low, Rona thought).

The skirt was huge and must have taken vast amounts of material. Emilia knew exactly how to use it, walking with a little flick of the hips that made it swirl provocatively. Only a supremely confident woman could have flaunted herself in this dress.

And Emilia was confident enough for anything, Rona thought. As she watched she saw the Russian start to twirl until she was like a crimson spinning top, laughing as she went. She came to a halt facing Rona, and her smile grew broader.

"Ah, the little English lady," she exclaimed. This was how she commonly referred to Rona, who was, in fact, slightly taller than most women. Rona had no doubt that it was a way of demeaning her.

Emilia's eyes swept over Rona's quiet clothes and her hair that said, 'governess'.

"How do you think I will look at Alice's ball?" she asked.

"You will look splendid, Countess," Rona replied quietly. "As you always do."

"Of course," said Emilia, sounding slightly shocked. "The important word is 'always'. A woman must always look her best. That is how to hold a man's interest. That and – other things."

She said the last words with a sly look that Rona found unbearable and her temper rose.

"I'm sure you are equally expert in the 'other things' madam," she said.

Emilia gave a tinkling laugh.

"Oh, my dear little governess, how unwise these people were to let you forget your station. It's so easy to get above yourself, isn't it? Easy to dream dreams of things that are impossible. How foolish of you!"

Rona's eyes glinted.

"You shouldn't be so easily deceived, madam. I am no governess, however it may look to you, and only I decide what is impossible."

A sudden tense look came into Emilia's eyes.

"No governess? In that case – what are you?"

Rona forced her common sense to return.

"Nothing," she said quickly.

"Oh come, you meant something by that."

"As you said madam, we all dream."

"And in your case – such sad little dreams. Oh, I know, my dear. I've followed your eyes. My poor brother deludes himself, doesn't he? Never mind, he'll get over it in time. And you – well, I don't care if you get over it or not, as long as you keep out of my way."

She stepped back and swirled her hips again, as if to emphasise her point.

"You will remember that, won't you?"

"I never forget anything, madam," said Rona deliberately. "Not a word, not a gesture – not an insult."

It was madness to speak in such a way, but at this moment she was facing the Countess as woman to woman and she could see, by Emilia's eyes, that she understood this.

"Are you so impertinent as to threaten me?"

"Yes," said Rona simply.

She had no idea what she would do if Emilia took up the challenge. She had said the words because her pride simply would not allow her to back down before this insolent creature. And she had her reward in the look of uncertainty that crossed Emilia's face.

The Russian recovered herself, but not completely. Her smile wavered a fraction, and she backed away until she reached the open door of the room where she had been changing. Then she turned her brilliant smile on somebody who was sitting in there, out of sight.

"Will I do, my darling? Are you getting your money's worth?"

Rona drew in a sharp breath.

She longed to know who was the man sitting in that room, the man who had paid to dress the Countess, and would presumably undress her.

But Emilia swung inside and shut the door firmly.

Rona remained outside, listening intently for the sound of voices.

But all she heard was soft male laughter, and she could not tell whose it was.

She stood there, watching that closed door, feeling the world go cold.

Suddenly she was frightened.

*

The great ballroom at the back of the Thierre house was festooned with white flowers. The orchestra was in place. Soon the guests would begin to arrive.

Upstairs everybody was in the last stages of preparation. Alice looked like a fairy in her white dress, her father's gift of pearls around her neck.

She had enjoyed a blissful birthday, except for one thing.

"If only Uncle Peter could have been here," she mourned. "How could he have forgotten my birthday?"

"Perhaps he's just very busy," Rona suggested, trying to sound unconcerned, although her own heart was sore.

She longed to see Peter, to look into his eyes and see there a denial of all the Countess had hinted. But he had not even bothered to return for Alice's birthday.

It was absurd to keep hoping. Now she knew all she had wanted to know.

For herself she had chosen a dress of pearl grey silk, as demure as the Countess was flamboyant. Its neck was

106

slightly higher than was normal for a ball gown. With it she wore a dainty silver filigree necklace, the most demure piece of jewellery she had taken with her.

She longed to dress up in her finest gown and most expensive jewels. She had been the belle of the ball in the past, and could be again, if only she were free to be herself.

But she was not free. She was the governess. She must never forget that.

The Earl frowned a little when he saw the dress, and she knew he was thinking how she would have looked in the one he had wanted to buy for her. But he had too much delicacy to refer to the matter again.

At last it was time for the ball to begin. Guests were arriving in luxurious carriages. Many of them were Monsieur Thierre's associates in government circles. It was a glittering occasion.

Monsieur Thierre himself opened the ball, dancing with Alice, while his wife danced with the Earl.

Rona was not short of partners. Henri danced with her, then Marcel and then Jacques, blushing furiously as he bowed before her.

Count Alexei appeared, full of good cheer, but unable to explain why his sister had not arrived.

"She has a life I know nothing about," he said with a wink at everyone. "I dare say she will be here soon."

He continued talking in this vein as he swept Rona around the floor. She answered mechanically, but afterwards she was glad to escape.

She was standing close to a door that stood ajar. It was a simple matter to slip through, praying that nobody would see her go.

Her prayers were answered, and she found herself in a broad corridor, lined with pictures on one side and large windows on the other.

It was blessedly peaceful to be alone, away from the hustle and bustle of admirers. If only she could get away from her own thoughts as easily. Would there ever be peace from her inner turmoil?

The windows looked out onto cloisters, with a lawn and a fountain. Coloured fairy lamps had been hung all around, giving the place a magical air. Rona stood watching the fountain, entranced by its beauty.

Then suddenly she grew very still.

She had seen something impossible.

The reflection of the spray was giving her illusions.

But the next moment she had found the door in the wall that led outside and was hurriedly pulling it open, then running through the cloisters, trying to see across the lawn to the arches beyond.

It was dark, but she knew she had seen him.

Harlequin.

He had been standing there, leaning against a pillar, his eyes gleaming through the slits of his mask.

But now he was gone.

She gave a little cry at the thought that she might have imagined him. He must be there, oh how could she endure this?

She turned a corner of the cloister, and then she saw the door opening at the far end. A hand reached out to beckon her. She hurried her steps but when she got there, the hand had gone.

The door was still open. Taking a deep breath she went into the darkened room beyond. What little she could see came from the coloured lights outside, but she could make out that the room was large and almost empty.

There was a click as the door closed behind her. She turned.

Harlequin stood there, looking at her.

"It's you," she whispered. "At least – is it?"

He came towards her, looking down on her in the gloom. The coloured lights emphasised the diamond pattern on his costume, but his mask, under the tricorne hat, hid the upper part of his face.

She could just make out his mouth, and her heart began to beat. It was the mouth she knew, wide, generous, and now smiling.

"Yes, it's me," he said softly. "I knew you would come."

"You said we would never meet again," she reminded him.

"I didn't dare hope that we would. It seemed so impossible. But I hadn't allowed for your courage in escaping."

"It was you who gave me courage," she said passionately. "I've often seemed to feel you beside me."

"That's because I've been there, always thinking of you – always with you."

"Why have you pretended not to know me?"

"I must. I have work to do, that must be done in secret. And you must tell nobody that we have met like this."

"But why?"

"Because it might put you in danger."

"In danger?" she echoed, truly surprised. "How can I be? Where does the danger come from?"

"Some of it comes from me," he answered unexpectedly. "I carry danger with me wherever I go. God forbid I should spread it to those I love. I had to see you tonight to warn you. Stay well clear of Rostoy. I cannot tell you why."

"Are you sure you aren't jealous?" she dared to ask.

She could just make out his smile.

"Should I be jealous of him?"

"Oh no, no!" she said eagerly. "I care nothing for him. Please, Peter – "

"Harlequin," he interrupted her quickly. "For us, Peter does not exist. It is better that way."

"But does Harlequin exist?"

He smiled again, in appreciation of her quick wit.

"He exists if you want him to," he said. "If he lives in your heart, then he exists. But you can dismiss him with a word or a sigh."

"I shall never say a word."

"I'm glad. Because I think, if you did, it would kill me."

"Please Harlequin, you must believe me when I say that Count Rostoy is nothing to me."

"I shall carry that assurance in my heart, just as I have carried you in my heart since that first night."

"There are so many things about you that I don't understand. The Russian Countess – "

Instantly his finger tips were over her mouth.

"Hush," he said sternly. "You must not ask me about her."

She drew a swift breath of dismay. His open flirting with the Countess, and perhaps more, was the one thing above all she longed to know about.

But there was suddenly an authority about him that contrasted oddly with the sprightly charm he normally displayed. Sometimes he seemed almost boyish, but at this moment he was a man, giving his commands, and expecting her to comply.

Rebellion rose in her. Why should he simply demand

obedience while he refused to explain?

"You are unfair to me," she burst out.

"I know," he said gravely. "This is hard on you, and unjust. But I have no choice. It all depends whether you can trust me totally, blindly. I have no right to ask it of you. I've given you every reason to be suspicious of me, and no reason to think well of me.

"I'm asking everything of you, and giving back very little – at this moment. But I hope the time may come when I can repay you with my whole heart.

"If you tell me that I ask too much I shall go away and never blame you. It is up to you."

Suddenly a new, vibrant note came into his voice.

"Tell me, my darling, can you trust me? Can you take that risk? And it is a terrible risk. More terrible than you can imagine. It will take all your courage and all the love of which you are capable."

Rona gazed at him, full of dread as she started to realise that something was happening that she could not begin to imagine – something fearful and outside her experience.

Something that might end in anguish and despair.

CHAPTER EIGHT

Rona faced him.

"I will trust you," she said fervently, "until the end of time."

"God bless you!"

"But is there nothing I may ask you?"

"Nothing."

"Not even why you ran away from the ball at Westminster House, when somebody called your name? Why did you conceal the fact that you were in London that night? Your brother-in-law thinks you arrived a day later."

"I know. So does everyone, and they must continue to believe it. My presence at that ball was unknown, and must remain so. Harlequin needs to come and go in secret."

"Then Harlequin too is in danger?"

This time his mouth stretched not in a smile but in a blazing grin. "Never fear. They can't catch me."

"But if they did?" she asked fearfully. "What would they do?"

"It doesn't matter because they never will. I'm protected by spells."

"Don't make a joke of it," she begged.

But now nothing could dim his jesting confidence.

"Don't you believe in magic?" Harlequin asked. "You should, because you weave spells of your own. You hold me in thrall at this very moment, and while your magic surrounds me, I am safe from the worst that the world can do."

"But can't you tell me – ?"

Swiftly his hand was across her mouth.

"No," he said seriously. "I can tell you nothing, except that you must believe in me. Is that so hard?"

"Not when you are here with me. But you will go again, and then I may be afraid, and lose faith."

"No, you will not," he said at once. "Because you are brave, and you know that I will never really leave you. And one day – "

"One day – ?" Rona whispered eagerly.

"One day, God willing, our time will come. In the mean time – "

He gathered her in his arms and pressed his lips to hers.

If she had doubted his identity before, she had no doubts now. His mouth was instantly familiar. This was the kiss she had dreamed of since that first kiss on another night, in another country.

That night at the ball now felt a lifetime ago. And yet the man was the same. Only she was different. The ignorant girl who had kissed him in the garden had been transformed since then into a woman with the confidence to take her life in her hands. Now that woman had found the man she loved, and nothing was going to stand in her way.

She kissed him back, pressing closer as his arms went around her and wrapping her own arms about him. She was his forever and she would believe in their ultimate union because she *must* believe it. Life would have no meaning for her otherwise.

He drew back and took her face in his hands, gazing down in the dim light. Distantly they could hear music coming from the ballroom.

"Dance with me," he whispered. "I cannot dance with you in front of the others. I would hold you too close, and reveal too much. If they saw us together everyone would know that you are the heart of my heart, and the light of my life."

"And I would want them to know that we love each other," she breathed. "I'd want to cry it to the world."

"One day we will. But not yet. First I have work that must be completed. When I have done my duty, then we will be free. Until then, dance with me, beloved."

The music reached them, sweet, aching, irresistible. He took her into his arms and began to move to the waltz. She closed her eyes and surrendered to him totally, following where he led, knowing only that she belonged to him, and would do so until the end of time.

At last the distant music stopped.

Again he took her face between his hands and looked searching at her.

"There are tears on your cheeks," he said. "Let me dry then."

He kissed her cheeks, her eyelids, her mouth, his lips lingering caressingly.

Then, suddenly, she was standing alone.

And when she opened her eyes, he was gone.

*

"Oh, Miss Johnson, there you are. I've been looking for you."

"I'm sorry Alice. I went out for some fresh air."

She had been away much too long, Rona realised. After Harlequin had left her, she could not face returning to the ballroom at once, so she had emerged into the cloisters and walked in the shadows until she felt more settled. Now she realised that she had been gone for an hour.

Alice had some news that she was longing to tell.

"Uncle Peter's here. Isn't that wonderful? I knew he wouldn't forget me. I should have trusted him, shouldn't I?"

"Yes," Rona said, smiling. "You should have trusted him."

The happiness of her brief time with Harlequin still pervaded her. She felt that she could face anything now.

But it was still hard when she reached the dance floor and saw Peter with the Countess in his arms. Emilia was wearing her crimson velvet dress, flaunting it, and herself, extravagantly. As they danced she smiled up at him in a sly, provocative way and her lips moved. He laughed and she spoke again, her lips dangerously close to his.

Had he been the man in her dressing room, the man who'd paid for the dress that was designed to be removed?

But this was something she must not ask. She had promised to trust him, and she would not fall at the first hurdle.

She put her head up, and made herself smile.

"Miss Johnson, at last!"

She turned to see the Earl, splendid in evening attire.

"I'm sorry, sir, I was just – "

"My dear, I wasn't demanding an explanation. It's just that your absence caused quite a commotion amongst the young men. They'll be bearing down on you any moment, so perhaps I could claim my dance first."

Smiling, she went into his arms and they circled the floor in a waltz.

"How very sedate you look," he said. "I suppose you were right to refuse my suggestion."

"I'm sure I was."

"You won't be offended if I say that you still outshine every woman here?"

"I'm not offended, sir, but it isn't true. Nor is it proper for you to speak so to your employee."

"Forgive me," he said at once. "You're right, no gentleman ought to – you're at a disadvantage and I shouldn't have – I apologise."

It was hard to believe that this shy man, so lacking in personal confidence, was an Earl. Beneath the trappings of his rank he was decent, kind and curiously humble. She thought she had never liked anyone so much.

She said something to reassure him and he smiled as though the sun had come out. He even had enough confidence to demand another dance.

The evening swirled on. She danced and laughed and talked. Once she even found herself talking to Peter. He bowed to her gallantly, asked if she was enjoying the evening, but he did not ask her to dance.

It was hard, now, to believe that her interlude with Harlequin had actually happened.

*

Everybody slept late next morning. When they awoke it became a lazy day of drifting around discussing the triumphs of the night before.

"I shall remember it all my life," sighed Alice ecstatically as the ladies were enjoying a leisurely lunch. "There were so many handsome young men who wanted to dance and flirt with me."

"Of course there were," said Rona. "And from now on, there will be many more. You are going to be the belle of a hundred balls."

Alice's eyes widened. Then she asked,

"Are you really and truly saying this will happen to me?"

"Of course it will," Rona replied. "But you must be

cautious, as you're still very young. And you must learn to be discriminating. When men pursue you, you have to decide whether they want you for yourself, or because your father is an Earl.

"Then one day, perhaps when you least expect it, you'll find a man who loves you just because you are you. He will adore you because you are the woman he's been looking for all his life."

"Oh, I can't wait," sighed Alice.

"You still have some work to do first. I think you know by now that knowing a language means not only that you understand the words someone is speaking, but what they are thinking and feeling. Sometimes they are not the same. A person might pretend great love for you, while secretly wondering what terms he can make."

"That's very true," said an unexpected voice, and they both looked up.

"Forgive me for listening to your private conversation," said the Earl, coming forward. "But I agreed with you so deeply that I had to join in. Some people speak loving words and think dark thoughts.

"But there are also others who think loving thoughts that they dare not voice. They speak of dull, every day things because they don't know how to tell someone what is in their hearts. So divining a person's true meaning can be as hard in your own language as in a foreign one."

"But surely," said Alice, "it would only be ladies who had to keep their feelings to themselves. A woman cannot tell a man that she loves him, but he can tell her."

"It's a convention that he can tell her," agreed her father. "But suppose the poor fellow is shy and tongue-tied, or maybe he feels that the lady is at a disadvantage, so he must treat her very carefully, for her sake?"

But these subtleties were beyond a very young girl

who'd just scored her first big social success. After puzzling for a moment she asked Rona,

"Miss Johnson, do you understand about that?"

"I understand this," Rona said. "What we all want, every one of us is love. If you are patient, you will find it. I assure you it is more precious than anything else in the whole world."

"I hope I fall in love very soon," sighed Alice.

"Now that is very silly of you," chided Rona lightly. "At your age you can afford to enjoy being a success. And don't forget, you haven't made your official debut yet. In England you will be presented at court, and have a coming out ball, and at least a year of parties and balls. It's great fun, and don't be in a hurry to cut it short."

She regretted saying "it's great fun" as soon as the words were out. Perhaps she would be lucky and nobody would notice the slip.

But then she looked up to see the Earl regarding her with a quiet interest in his eyes.

*

Dinner was an informal meal that night. Everyone was still feeling the after effects of the night before. Now the men had returned home and again the talk was of the ball.

Monsieur Thierre was arguing that Alice's success was a reason for a longer visit. She must stay for at least another month. His wife backed him.

The Earl agreed to another week, but after that he was determined to go home.

"At this rate, when we return the dog will bark at us thinking we're strangers," he joked.

Everybody laughed. Then something strange happened.

As the laughter died, they could hear noises coming

from the hall outside. Voices were raised in protest, but above them all came one voice that Rona thought she knew. Suddenly her blood ran cold. It was impossible, surely?

"My dear Rona, whatever is the matter?" the Earl asked her urgently. "You've gone white."

"Nothing, I – I'm sure it's nothing," she stammered.

"But it must be something very grave to make you look so ill." He laid his hand gently over hers. "Please tell me. Perhaps I can help."

The noise was getting louder. Now there was no doubt that it was her father's voice.

"How could he have found me?" she whispered. "Oh, this is terrible. I can't bear it."

His hand tightened on hers.

"Tell me what you want me to do," he said.

"There is nothing you can do. Nobody can save me."

"My dear girl, save you from what? Tell me, I'll do anything."

Monsieur Thierre had risen from his seat and started towards the door. The Earl also rose, looking at the door.

Rona's mind whirled. In just a few moments her fate would be sealed, and her head was full of confusion.

She could not prevent herself looking across at Peter. He alone had heard her father's voice before, and would understand what was happening. He had come to her aid before, and her heart had never forgotten.

But what would he do now?

Would this man, who still seemed at the Countess's feet, despite what he had said to her last night, want to trouble himself about her desperate situation?

She half expected to find him so engrossed in the Countess that he had no attention for herself, but he was gazing across the table at her, with something in his face that she could not read.

It was as if he were possessed by horror. His face was very pale and his eyes seemed almost aghast. Then his expression changed and a kind of resigned despair seemed to settle over him.

The next moment the door to the dining room was flung violently open, and James Trafford stood on the threshold.

His face was dark with fury as he took in the room. At last his gaze came to rest on Rona.

"So there you are," he snapped.

"Papa – "

Ignoring her cry he spoke in a harsh voice.

"Who is the master here?"

Monsieur Thierre stepped forward.

"My name is Armand Thierre, and this is my house. You are – ?"

"I am James Trafford. You must forgive me for disturbing you when you are having a meal, but I have come to fetch my daughter back to England. It was only last night that I was told where she was staying in Paris, otherwise I would have been here earlier."

Rona gave a murmur of horror and felt as if she was turned into stone.

Monsieur Thierre gave a little bow and addressed the intruder with exquisite courtesy.

"You are welcome in my house, Mr. Trafford," he said, and held out his hand.

Mr. Trafford ignored it and strode the length of the table until he reached Rona. He snapped,

"You have put me to a great deal of trouble to find you.

Now go upstairs and pack your case. I am taking you back to England."

For a moment Rona could only stare at him. Then she summoned up her courage and said,

"I am sorry, but I prefer to stay here."

"You are coming back to England with me immediately," her father answered angrily. "You have behaved in a disgraceful manner in running away and you will marry Lord Robert as soon as we get home."

"I am not coming home, Papa," Rona replied, as firmly as she could. "I am engaged as a governess. I am very happy in my employment."

"Stuff and nonsense!" her father exclaimed. "You are no more a governess than I am. You are engaged to Lord Robert and you will conduct yourself with propriety. You had no right to run away in that scandalous manner causing both me and him a great deal of trouble. Go upstairs at once, do you hear me?"

There was silence, as though nobody knew what to do. He was speaking in English, but the guests around the table were all cultivated people, and knew enough of the language to understand what was happening.

Then the Earl who had been staring with astonishment at Mr. Trafford, said,

"I think, sir, you are being, to say the least of it, somewhat offensive. Your daughter is employed by me as a governess, and I would be very sorry to lose her."

Mr. Trafford stared at him and said sharply: "If my daughter is pretending to be a governess, it is all part of her disgraceful behaviour in running away from home and from the man she is to marry."

Rona sprang to her feet.

"No! No! No!" she cried. "I will not do that. I will not

marry Lord Robert whatever you say."

"You are my daughter, and you will do what I tell you to do."

"I will not marry him! I will not!" Rona exclaimed angrily.

Now there were tears in her eyes and her words came shakily.

It was then the Earl went to stand beside Rona.

"Your daughter is remaining here," he said.

"You should be silent, sir," Mr. Trafford thundered. "You have no standing in this matter."

"On the contrary. My standing is that of her promised husband."

Rona gasped and stared at him, uncertain whether she had heard correctly.

"What do you mean?" Mr. Trafford asked sharply.

"What I say," the Earl answered. "Your daughter has promised to be my wife."

Silence.

"My daughter, sir, is engaged to another man."

"No," said the Earl quietly. "She is not."

"How dare you – "

"It is her decision, not yours. I will not permit you to bully her or take her away against her will."

"*You* will not permit – ? You have absolutely no authority – "

"I am Rona's fiancé. This is my authority, and I shall exercise it to the full to stop her being upset in any way. There is, after all, no reason why you should forbid the marriage."

"Forbid it, of course I forbid it!" Mr. Trafford said angrily. "I have made other plans for her."

"But they are not *my* plans," said Rona desperately.

She understood now that the Earl had made this desperate gamble to save her, but would not expect her to take him seriously. Once her father had departed, things would resume their normal course. All she had to do was play her part.

Her heart ached a little that it was not Peter who had exerted himself to save her. But he was standing close to the Countess, half turned away from Rona. She had the feeling that he was deliberately avoiding looking at her. Her anger flared, and it gave her courage.

"You should listen to her," said the Earl gravely. "If she is set against this man, you surely cannot expect to force her."

"She is my daughter and I demand her obedience. I have her best interests at heart, and have arranged a good marriage for her – a man with a title – "

"A Duke perhaps?" enquired the Earl with cool courtesy. "Or a Marquis?"

These were the only two titles that outranked his own.

"A connection to a Duke," said Rona's father stiffly.

"Oh Papa!" she exclaimed in despair. "He's a younger son, and he has no hope of the title, because if he had he wouldn't be bothering with me."

"Then he's a great fool," said the Earl, smiling at her. "Sir – " he returned his attention to Mr Trafford, "I should have introduced myself before. I am the Earl of Lancing, and it will be my pleasure – my honour – to make Rona my Countess. I know that I shall be happy with her, and I shall do my best to make her happy with me."

At that, the guests broke into applause. All around the table people were smiling, looking from Rona to the Earl, then back to the outraged father.

Mr. Trafford reacted to this announcement very curiously. He should have been pleased at the prospect of this advancement for his daughter, but the scowl did not leave his face.

Rona, knowing her father, guessed that his chief emotion at this moment was fury at being defied. He had decreed that she should marry Lord Robert, and he wanted his own way, even in the face of a better prospect for her.

He glared at the Earl.

"I will consider your application for my daughter's hand," he said stiffly. "I am far from certain that you would be a suitable husband for her. In the meantime she must come with me."

"No," said the Earl quietly.

He guessed, as did Rona, that once she was in her father's power there would be no escape again. This man was too angry to think clearly.

Mr. Trafford's next act confirmed it. He shot out a hand to grasp Rona's wrist.

"You will come with me," he raged, trying to pull her to her feet.

But he was thwarted by the Earl's hand on his arm. Looking around he saw that every man in the room had closed in behind him.

"Come to see me tomorrow," said the Earl, "and we will discuss arrangements, settlements and so forth. I love your daughter, and you will not find me ungenerous. But for the moment I think you should leave. Perhaps later your natural fatherly affection will enable you to wish us happiness."

For a moment Mr. Trafford stared at his daughter, then at the Earl. His face was black with fury.

Then he turned sharply round and walked from the room.

He slammed the door behind him and for a moment no one moved.

Then uproar broke out. There was more applause and a few cheers. Monsieur Thierre signalled to the butler, and within moments footmen began bringing in champagne.

Alice was in ecstasies.

"Oh, I'm so happy. Now you'll stay with us for always."

"No, no, darling, you don't understand," Rona said frantically. "It isn't real. Your Papa said that in order to protect me, but he didn't mean it."

"Did I not mean it?" the Earl asked her quizzically.

"My Lord, please, you mustn't think – I know very well that you were only being kind. Please don't imagine that I'll try to take advantage by holding you to it."

He took both her hands in his and spoke gravely. "I know that you are the most honourable woman in the world, far too honourable to take advantage of me. Perhaps it is I who has taken advantage of you."

He smiled at her warmly.

"You had to choose between returning with that dreadful bully of a father, or accepting my hand. My dear, what a terrible choice. How unfair for you to be put in that position! We will say no more for now. Let them drink to us if they want to, and then you and I will talk privately together later. Never fear. Nobody will force you to do anything you don't like. I won't allow that."

Rona heard these gentle words with astonishment. For the first time it dawned on her that the Earl was following his heart. He actually wanted to marry her.

Looking into his eyes she saw warmth and tender devotion.

And love.

Rona was shaken to the depths by the discovery.

This generous man loved her, and suddenly her situation was not simple after all.

"Do you know what I think?" he asked lightly. "I think the best thing either of us can do is to simply go along with this for as long as necessary."

"But think what a position you're putting yourself in," she urged. "If I were unscrupulous, I could sue you for breach of promise."

He smiled tenderly.

"Now, why didn't it occur to me that you might be unscrupulous?" he asked. "But you know, my dear Miss Johnson, I feel strangely safe putting my fate in your hands."

His eyes were glowing with love for her. She wanted to turn away from the beauty of that glow. He was such a good man, and she felt as guilty as if she was deliberately deceiving him. But she was trapped, with no escape.

CHAPTER NINE

"My real name is Rona Trafford. The man who burst in here is my father, and he's trying to force me to marry Lord Robert Horton. I'll die first."

Rona was sitting with the Earl in the library of the Thierre house. The evening was over and their hosts had kindly left them alone.

"I've met Lord Robert," the Earl mused. "Cannington's son. I've never liked him, or his father, come to that. From what I hear he needs an heiress."

"Exactly," said Rona bitterly. "Lord Robert wants me only for my father's money, but he's been making love to a friend of mine. Insofar as he has a heart at all, it belongs to her. But he abandoned her, so that he could court me.

"When I found out the truth, I was determined to do anything to get away. Then I saw your advertisement in the newspaper. Forgive me for deceiving you."

"There is nothing to forgive," the Earl said at once. "I think you were very brave. Of course this explains everything about you that has puzzled me."

Rona gave a faint smile.

"Yes, I didn't play the part very convincingly, did I?"

"Well, you're like no other governess I've ever met, but my family is so much happier since you joined it. I think your father will never give up until we announce an official engagement."

"Please don't worry about that, my Lord – "

"But I'm not worried. It's what I hope for. Of course, from your point of view it's a very poor match. I'm a lot older than you, and I know you're not in love with me, as I am with you. But if you have nowhere else to go then perhaps – you might consider becoming my wife."

Rona gazed at him, touched by the humility with which he described himself as a poor match, and was prepared to accept second best.

"You would marry a woman who is not in love with you?" she asked at last.

"I love you so much I would care for nothing else. You could have anything you wanted to make you happy."

Now she must tell him that it was hopeless because she loved his brother-in-law. But that would involve explanations that she could not make. Her promise to Peter held her silent.

"Don't answer now," the Earl said. "We have until tomorrow to decide how to confront your father."

His tone was so kind that her conscience tortured her. Surely she might give him just a hint of the truth, to save him suffering? Peter would understand.

And then Peter walked into the library.

Overjoyed, Rona looked into his face, trying to read there some sign that she might speak. But the Earl spoke first.

"Peter, I'm glad you came."

"That was quite a speech you made in there, old boy," Peter observed.

"I meant every word of it. I've just been telling Rona how much I love her and long to marry her. I can tell you, because you're family. You don't mind, do you – about Valerie?"

From outside the library came the sound of Emilia's

voice, advancing on them.

Rona had the feeling that Peter pulled himself together.

"Valerie has been dead for four years, Giles," he said in a voice that revealed nothing. "I'm glad for anything that makes you happy. Is it settled?"

"Good heavens, no! Rona hasn't made her decision and since her position is delicate, I think we'd better leave matters until the morning."

But the Earl's looks belied his words. He was glowing with joy.

"Oh, you poor darling!"

Emilia stood in the doorway, in a froth of theatrical sympathy. She darted across the room to touch Rona on the cheek.

"How terrible for you! But how delightful that everything has ended so happily. And now you will be Lady Lancing."

"She will if I have my way," said the Earl warmly.

"Then I wish you both very happy," said Emilia at once, kissing Rona on both cheeks.

Rona felt stunned. A great tidal wave was carrying her onwards and she could do nothing to stop it. Whatever help she had expected from Peter was not going to be forthcoming. She knew that now.

She had a stark choice.

Return to her father, to be bullied into marriage with a man she despised.

Or marry this warm-hearted man who loved her, although she did not love him. Ally herself with Peter by marriage, and endure the torment of loving him hopelessly all her life.

"I'm very tired," she said hurriedly.

"Of course you must go to bed," said the Earl at once.

"And you and I must go out dancing," Emilia told Peter. "Come, you promised me."

"And I never break a promise to a lady," he said lightly.

But he could not look at Rona while he said it.

*

Rona rose early and dressed quietly so as not to wake Alice, and slipped downstairs to the garden, and from there to the little wood beyond. She desperately needed to be alone to weep.

She had wept during the night, but had smothered her sobs in the pillow, so that Alice should not hear.

She felt alone and adrift as never before. She did not understand anything that was happening to her. All she knew was that nothing made sense, and the man she had loved and trusted had abandoned her.

She walked under the trees for a long time, thinking of the day ahead. Soon her father would be here, and she and the Earl would continue the pretence of an engagement.

And afterwards?

The future was a blank.

"Rona."

She looked round quickly, but as first she could see nothing but trees. The sound was a whisper that seemed to come from nowhere.

"Rona."

It was the voice of the man she loved. Then she saw him walking towards her through the trees. In that moment everything was forgotten but the fact that she loved him and she ran to him, her arms opened wide.

His own arms opened to her. She flung herself into

them and they stood motionless for a long time, clasping each other, heart to heart and soul to soul.

"I had to come and find you," he said at last, "to say goodbye."

"Why does it have to be goodbye?" she asked huskily.

"Because of Giles. Did you see how he looked at you? If only I could have stepped in last night, there might have been a chance for us."

"Why didn't you?" she cried.

"Because I couldn't," he cried. "It tortured me not to be the one to help you, but I have a duty to others that made it impossible. I couldn't put myself first. I couldn't put you first. I wanted to but I *couldn't*. Try to understand, I beg you – "

"How can I understand something you won't tell me about? What is this duty you speak of? Are you married."

"No," he said violently. "And I never will be now. Nobody, if not you." He forced himself to calm down. "And now I know that it cannot be you. After Giles said so much in front of everyone – "

He stopped. His voice was shaking.

"He's the best man in the world," he went on after a while. "He's always been good to me. A few years ago I was wild. I got into bad company, and then into trouble. Giles hauled me out and set me straight again. It wasn't just to make my sister happy. She was dead by then, and couldn't have been hurt.

"Giles stood by me because he was my friend. No man ever had a better friend. But for him I wouldn't be here now. He has never asked me for anything in return. I can't repay him by behaving like a cad."

He groaned suddenly. "I had no idea how much he loved you."

"Neither had I," she said wretchedly. "And when he came to my rescue last night – my father would have dragged me away by force. He had authority on his side. Who could have stopped him using it?"

"Nobody except your promised husband," Peter said sombrely. "As you say, he rescued you. Having accepted his protection, you cannot throw it back in his face."

"I know," Rona said. "It would mean exposing him to public derision."

"We can't do that to him," Peter said harshly. "When we leave each other now, it will be forever. But first – kiss me, my darling, kiss me again – and again – "

She wept as she kissed him. She had enjoyed so brief a love, and it was over almost before it had begun. Now she felt as though her life was over too, and all she would have left would be the fleeting echo of a love that had once nearly happened.

But she knew there was no choice. They could not build their happiness on the pain of a man who had deserved well of both of them. No matter how much they might long to be together, their honour forbade it.

So she kissed him passionately but with finality. And then she wrenched herself from his arms and fled temptation.

On the edge of the wood she took one last look back, and saw him standing where she had left him. He was quite still, his eyes fixed on her. Then she turned and ran into the house.

And she did not look back again.

*

Her father arrived at precisely eleven o'clock. He was shown ceremoniously into the library, where Rona and the Earl were waiting for him.

A change had come over Mr. Trafford since the night

before. He smiled, even if briefly. He shook hands with the Earl and nodded to Rona.

"My dear," he said gruffly.

Rona felt as though she were in a trance. In a few moments her life would be settled.

But was it really too late? She had still not given the Earl her formal answer.

But then she felt his hand take hers as though seeking reassurance. She could not hurt him. If she had not known it before, she knew it now.

She squeezed his hand back, and smiled at him.

"I take it the matter is settled," said Mr. Trafford abruptly.

The Earl looked at Rona.

"Yes," she said. "It is settled."

"With your permission, sir," said the Earl with a little bow, "I should like to make Miss Trafford my wife, the Countess of Lancing."

"Very well," Mr. Trafford barked. "You are so determined that I suppose you know that I'm a rich man."

"Papa!" Rona exclaimed.

"Miss Trafford's dowry is unimportant to me," Lord Lancing said. "Until last night I did not know who she was. If she were penniless, I should still want her to be mine."

Mr. Trafford snorted in derision. Rona wanted to sink with shame.

The Earl mentioned settlements. The talk became financial. Rona ceased to listen. She felt the cage closing around her.

At last it was over. Her father rose to his feet, crossed the floor and kissed her forehead.

"My dear child, I am happy for you," he said in a voice

that sounded forced. "As soon as we're back in London I'll give a big engagement party for you. Now, go and pack."

"What?" she looked at him.

"Go and pack. We are returning to London together."

"No," she said at once.

The smile remained on his face but behind it his teeth were gritted.

"Go upstairs and pack immediately. Now that you are betrothed it is highly improper for you to live under the same roof as your fiancé."

"Not at all," Rona replied. "We aren't alone in the house, and it is not improper."

"We'll all be returning to England in a couple of days – " the Earl began.

"And I repeat that my daughter must return with me. Until you are married she owes me the obedience of a daughter. No doubt you will wish your wife to obey you!"

"No," said the Earl immediately. "I should hope that my wife would try to please me out of affection, just as I should with her."

Mr. Trafford snorted.

"I've no time to argue. Rona!"

"No," she said firmly. "I'm staying here."

In the silence that followed the Earl took a step towards her, silently signalling that she was under his protection now.

Mr. Trafford looked from one to the other, and his face hardened.

"In that case," he barked, "I will see you in London."

He turned and walked out.

"You see?" said the Earl in triumph. "When he was faced with us both, he had to give in."

"Yes, he does seem to have done," said Rona doubtfully.

The Earl took a large and very beautiful diamond ring from his pocket. He slipped it onto her finger and then carried her hand to his lips.

"My dear wife," he said reverently.

*

Later that day Rona wandered out into the garden again. She needed solitude before she could face the world.

She had no right to feel wretched.

She was betrothed to a good man, who wanted to make her happy.

And in time she might learn to forget the feel of Peter's passionate lips on hers, the glory of his love. Maybe one day she would no longer remember what might have been.

One day.

When she was dead.

She had wandered into the wood where they had said their last farewells that morning. Her feet took her to the very same spot, and she closed her eyes. Here, hidden by the trees, she would say goodbye to him in her heart.

Then she heard a noise.

For a wild, joyful moment she allowed herself to hope.

But when she opened her eyes it was her father standing there.

"Papa," she faltered. "I thought you had gone."

"I returned to fetch you," he grated.

"But – "

He seized her wrist.

"Do you think I was fooled by that little scene in there? He has no intention of marrying you."

"Of course he has or he would never have talked to

you," she cried, frantically trying to free herself.

"He'll keep you abroad, wandering around Europe, having his way with you, then toss you aside before he returns to England. Who'll care for your reputation if I don't?"

"You don't care for my reputation," she said angrily. "You're just set on having your own way, whatever it does to me."

"Now listen here my girl, you may think the chance of being a Countess is glorious, but the Duke of Cannington has made me certain offers – his friendship, membership of his clubs, a position in court circles, a title – "

"All of which he'll forget the minute he's secured your money for his son."

"Lancing couldn't do any of that, even if he wanted to. He never goes anywhere, shuns society. He doesn't even go to Ascot. Cannington's son is my choice."

"But not mine," she cried as he dragged her away. "Let me go Papa! Help!"

She tried to scream again but her father's hand was over her mouth. He was dragging her irresistibly through the trees to where she could see a wall, with a wrought iron gate in it, through which she could see a closed carriage.

There was a man on the other side of the gate, watching them approach. He opened the gate so that Mr. Trafford was able to haul her through without taking his hand from her mouth. Then the man opened the door of the carriage and the two of them thrust her in.

Her father got in after her and the vehicle began to move. Desperately she tried to get out the other side, but that door was locked.

"Sit down and stop your nonsense," he grated. "You're coming with me and that's that."

"No," she cried. "No, Papa please let me go."

"Shut up!" he said.

But she fought him like a mad thing, refusing to give up. The cab was going faster and faster, rocking from side to side. In his fury her father raised his hand. In another moment he would have struck her, but suddenly the carriage lurched more violently than ever.

He lost his balance, falling against the locked door. The carriage righted itself, sending Rona against the other door, which opened under the impact. She went flying out onto the pavement and picked herself up, running desperately.

From behind her she heard her father's angry voice, shouting for her to come back. It only made her run faster. If she did not escape now, she knew there would never be another chance.

And then, just up ahead, she saw her salvation.

"Alexei," she screamed. "Alexei, help me!"

The Russian Count was mounted on a big black horse. He turned at the sound of her voice, and nothing had ever looked so welcome to her as his splendid moustache.

"My dear girl," he roared. "Whatever has happened?"

"Help me. Please just help me escape."

"Come!"

He reached down, wrapped an arm around her waist and hauled her up before him. The next moment they were galloping down the street, away from her father, to safety.

*

"But she cannot simply have vanished," the Earl cried in distraction. "Who saw her last?"

"One of the maids saw her go into the garden," said Madame Thierre. "It seems that nobody has seen her since then. We thought she was in her room, but Alice says this is not so."

"But that was two hours ago," said the Earl, aghast. "We must search for her."

"My friend," said Monsieur Thierre, "we have already combed the house and gardens, and she is not there. Alice says that none of her things is missing. It would appear that she did not leave willingly."

"My God!" said the Earl, turning pale. "That father of hers – surely it isn't possible – ?"

But Peter, entering the house from the garden, confirmed the worst.

"I've been talking to a lad outside your rear gate," he said. "Earlier today he saw a young woman being forced into a carriage. From the description it sounds like Rona."

"And he didn't raise the alarm?" demanded the Earl, aghast.

"He's rather a slow-witted lad," said Peter. "He didn't think anything of it until I started asking questions."

"He's had two hours' head start," the Earl groaned. "If he took the train he'll be at Calais by now."

"But perhaps he didn't," said Monsieur Thierre. "A timetable, quickly, from my study."

Marcel hurried to the study and appeared a moment later with the timetable, which his father studied with satisfaction.

"It is as I thought," he said. "There was no train to Calais this afternoon. The next one is this evening. He won't have risked such a delay. It's more likely that he's heading for the coast in that carriage, in which case you can overtake him on horseback. Take my fastest horses."

"I'll come with you," said Marcel at once.

"And I," said Henri. "If he tries to hold on to her, you

may need our help."

The four men set out ten minutes later, galloping out of Paris with fierce, determined faces. As Monsieur Thierre had prophesied, they overtook the slow carriage after only an hour, and converged on it like bandits.

Marcel and Henri seized the horses' bridles, while the Earl and Peter opened the door to confront the man inside.

But he was alone.

Peter's face was livid. "Where is she?" he demanded. "What have you done with her?"

"Nothing," shouted Mr. Trafford. "She escaped me and now I'm done with her."

"Where did she escape you?" demanded the Earl in a terrible voice. "Tell us where to look for her."

"How do I know? She's in Paris somewhere. I'd only had her a few minutes when she managed to get out of the door. I saw her hurl herself straight into the arms of the first man she saw, like any hussy."

"What do you mean?" demanded Peter. "What man?"

"I never saw him before, but he had a big moustache. He just swept her up on to his horse. Good riddance, I say! I'm returning to England, and she can save herself from whatever mess she's got into. She's no daughter of mine. Now, let go of me."

Slowly Peter released the man's coat.

Mr. Trafford pulled the door shut and the carriage rumbled away.

"Count Rostoy," said the Earl. "Thank goodness she's safe."

"Is she safe?" demanded Peter. "Doesn't it occur to you that if he rescued her in Paris he had time enough to return her to us? It was many hours ago."

"Peter, for pity's sake, what are you saying? She went

to him as a friend. He'll protect her."

"Then why hadn't he brought her home when we left? Or sent us a message to say she was safe?"

The Earl paled.

"You don't think – ? But he seems such a decent fellow, and he wouldn't risk a scandal, surely?"

"He wouldn't care. He isn't planning to be in Paris long. He's not a decent fellow, Giles. He plays the buffoon, but he's actually one of the most dangerous men in Europe."

Peter vaulted onto his horse.

"Come on," he called to the others. "We haven't a moment to lose."

CHAPTER TEN

At first there was nothing to alarm Rona. When she asked Alexei why he wasn't taking her straight back to the Thierres' house he replied,

"That man who kidnapped you – "

"My father – "

"Yes, your father. He may return there and try to seize you again. It's better if I take you to my home and send them a message."

It made sense. She preferred to be in a place that her father did not know about.

She knew that Alexei and Emilia lived in a large, expensive hotel, but instead of heading there he took her into streets she had never heard of.

"Where are we going?" she asked.

"To a place where you will be safe," he replied.

The house, when they reached it, was small and shabby. Rona was puzzled, but not yet worried.

"You can rest here," Alexei said, leading her inside, "while I send a message to your friends. Why don't you lie down. You've had a bad shock. The maid will bring you some tea."

He gave her into the hands of a middle-aged maid, who showed her upstairs to a small bedroom. It was shabby but neat and clean, and a few minutes later the maid brought tea, as Alexei had promised.

It was when she had drunk the tea that Rona began to sense something wrong. Almost at once her head began to swim. The room seemed to advance and retreat around her and darkness crept over her senses. Her last conscious thought was that she had walked out of one trap into another.

When she woke she was alone. Through the window she could see that the light had faded, meaning that some hours had passed since she had been brought here and drugged.

But why? She thought frantically.

She knew why her father had kidnapped her, but why had Alexei done this? She had regarded him as a friend.

She got to her feet, feeling light headed but apart from that, well enough, and made her way to the door. As she had half expected, it was locked.

But almost as soon as she had sat down again there was a noise outside, the door opened, and Emilia came in.

"What does all this mean?" Rona asked. "Why have you brought me here?"

The beautiful Russian shrugged.

"It's a little sooner than Alexei and I had intended, but no matter. You fell into our hands, and in our trade you can't overlook your opportunities."

"Your – trade? What is that?"

"Come, don't play ignorant with me. We're in the same trade. You virtually admitted it that day we met in the gown shop. 'I am no governess, however it may look.' Those were your words. You made the mistake of getting angry, and anger loosens the tongue."

Rona was on the verge of saying that she had been talking about her flight from her father, when something held her back. There was a mystery here, and this woman thought she already knew it. That meant she could be tempted into talking. Rona took a long, slow breath.

"How incautious of me," she said lightly. "Otherwise I don't believe you would have ever seen through me."

Emilia nodded.

"Not for a while, at any rate. You're good at your job, I'll give you that. Our Embassy in London sent a message to say that British Intelligence had put one of its best operatives on to us, but couldn't tell us who it was. We've been trapped here in Paris while we waited to get our hands on the other half, watching every step, always wondering who knew our secret."

"Well," said Rona with a smile, "now you know it was me."

It was like fencing in the dark, feint and parry, trying to see behind her enemy's eyes. But she was learning many things. And now, incredibly, she thought she understood the secret that Peter could never tell.

"I always felt there was something suspicious about you," said Emilia. "My husband disagreed."

Just in time Rona stopped herself saying "your husband?"

Of course. It was growing clearer by the minute.

She managed to shrug and say casually,

"By 'your husband', of course, you mean Alexei. That was always fairly obvious. You weren't as clever as you thought."

Emilia's face darkened. "Don't make the mistake of sneering at me."

"Good heavens, why not? You haven't been very clever from start to finish. Only a fool would have been taken in by that brother and sister act."

Emilia regarded her.

"So you knew Alexei was married all the time you were making eyes at him?"

"In this business we all have our own methods," Rona said with a smile that was calculated to infuriate the other woman.

By the sudden hardening of Emilia's face she guessed she had succeeded.

"Peter was taken in," Emilia snapped.

Rona's shrug was a masterpiece of indifference. Part of her was afraid, but another part was full of a thrilling excitement. Now the pieces were falling into place one by one, and she knew almost everything.

"What does Peter matter?" she asked. "I wasn't taken in by it."

"I'm not sure how much Peter does matter," Emilia said, considering. "Alexei has always thought that he was the operative who was after us."

"Oh no," said Rona quickly. "Not him. Me. Your instincts are better than Alexei's."

"Unless, of course, you're both working for British Intelligence."

Rona's heart was beating urgently, but she managed to appear calm as she shook her head.

"Really," she said. "To suggest that I need his help is practically an insult. Two of us would be quite needless."

Emilia nodded. "Yes, while we have you, there's no need to search further."

"So, that just leaves the problem of 'the other half'," Rona said, taking up the phrase Emilia had used before, although she had no idea what it meant. "I imagine you've taken care of that by now."

"Oh yes, but only since this morning. We're ready to leave for Russia as soon as it gets dark."

"And me?"

"Why, you'll come with us, of course. There are people in St. Petersburg who will be eager to talk to you."

"But suppose I don't wish to talk to them?"

"You will – in the end. They will persuade you."

Rona refused to reply to this, but fear was curling inside her. They could take her away to Russia, where she would come to a miserable end, and nobody would ever know.

How would the Earl and Peter know where to look for her? If they ever guessed the truth, it would be too late.

But he would be safe. She would cling to that thought. She would die, if necessary, clinging to the thought of his safety.

"I'll get you something to eat," said Emilia.

"No thank you. I'm not falling for that again."

"But I think you should have something."

Emilia vanished, locking the door.

Alone, Rona began to study the room more closely. There was one window through which she could see a garden with trees.

As she had expected, the window was locked, but the wood was old and rotten. Taking a deep breath, she aimed a punch at the frame and the wood splintered, taking the lock with it. Now she could push open the window and see out further.

As evening drew on the light was fading, but she could just make out dark shapes under the trees. Evidently the sound of the window breaking had alerted them for they were looking up.

Rona bit back a cry of joy as she recognised Peter's face. Behind him there were several other figures.

Swiftly Peter put a finger to his lips. Then he began to

climb the tree nearest the wall until he was opposite the window. Rona pushed open the other side to give him the biggest possible way in, but it was still going to be tight.

Neither did the tree come quite close enough to be useful. Peter inched along the branch as far as he could, but when he reached out, his hand still came a few inches short of the wall. The most he could manage was to stretch out his leg until his foot fitted onto the window sill.

Rona leaned out to him.

"Hurry," she said. "They must have heard the noise. Take my hand."

With one hand she steadied herself against the wall while the other hand reached out to him. He grasped it.

"Now," he said and launched himself forward.

At the same moment Rona threw herself back, pushing against the wall with her other hand, so that their combined momentum hurled him through the window.

They landed on the floor together, breathing hard but triumphant.

"They must have heard us," she said.

"Have they hurt you?" he demanded, taking hold of her and looking anxiously into her face.

"No, just a drugged cup of tea which I've slept off. But they plan to move out tonight, taking me with them. They think I'm working for British Intelligence, but it's you, isn't it?"

He nodded. "I'll never forgive myself for letting you run into danger, but I never thought of anything like this. Why does Emilia think it's you?"

"Some trivial remark which she misunderstood. Listen, someone's coming."

There were footsteps on the stair. They both got to their feet and Peter positioned himself behind the door. The next moment Emilia unlocked the door and marched in.

"What was – ?"

She had no time to say more. In what seemed to be one movement Peter seized her from behind, tossed her onto the bed, grabbed Rona's hand and pulled her through the door, which he locked behind them.

"Now, let's get you out of here," he said.

"I think not," came a voice from below.

Downstairs in the hall stood Count Alexei, smiling from behind his moustache, as always. But now there was something different about his smile. There was no humour, only bared teeth. And in his hand was a wicked looking pistol.

From the front door behind him came the sound of pounding and shouts. The locked door shook under the thundering fists.

"Come down," said Alexei. "Both of you."

"You have nowhere to go," Peter told him. "Listen to that noise. Do you think they'll let you go?"

Alexei's genial mask had fallen away leaving behind the man's true face, cold, deadly. His eyes, which had always seemed full of humour, were blank.

"What they allow me to do, and what I do are two different things," he said. "Come down. Her first." With the pistol he indicated Rona.

What happened next was too fast for her to follow. She felt Peter move, shielding her with his body and pushing her violently so that she fell to the floor. In the same moment the front door crashed in and the Earl, Henri and Marcel streamed into the hall, reaching out to grab Alexei.

But he was too fast for them. Raising his arm he fired high on the stairs.

There was a deafening explosion. Peter staggered,

clutching his shoulder, then fell and rolled to the bottom of the stairs.

Rona screamed.

"Oh God! Peter – Peter – !"

The next moment she was flying down the stairs to fall on her knees beside his still form.

"No," she wept. "No – please – no!"

His eyes were closed, his face deathly white.

"Peter," she whispered. "Peter, my love. Don't leave me. I love you so much."

Henri and Marcel hurled Alexei to the floor, disarmed him and tied his hands.

Still Peter did not move. Oblivious of all others, Rona raised his bleeding form in her arms and cradled it against her in a passion of grief.

It couldn't happen, she thought wildly. How could God be so cruel?

"Peter, Peter," she whispered in agony, rocking him back and forth.

She looked up, choking back her tears.

"He's still alive," she said. "For pity's sake, get a doctor. Oh Peter, Peter – please God, no!"

Unseen, the Earl turned away, hiding his face in his hands.

Rona was never able to sort out the details of what happened then. Not only the Thierre sons but Monsieur Thierre himself and two hefty servants were there. One went for a doctor and one for the Chief of Police, who was a good friend of Monsieur Thierre, and accepted his explanation about the Russians.

"They are spies, wanted both here and in England. Keep them safe and the appropriate authorities will be in touch with you. With any luck you should get a medal."

By the time Emilia and Alexei had been hauled away, the doctor was examining Peter's wound.

"High up on the shoulder," he said. "But it missed the lung, or he wouldn't be alive."

"Will he live?" asked the Earl tensely.

"I believe so, with proper care. But he can't stay here."

"My carriage is outside," said Monsieur Thierre. "I took the precaution of bringing it to take Rona home. Now we will take Peter."

"He must be kept warm," said the doctor.

Rona sped upstairs for blankets. The Earl took some from her and together they wrapped Peter in them. Despite the doctor's reassuring words, his face was a frightening colour. Rona kept her terrified eyes fixed on him, only closing them for a brief moment of prayer.

"Please," she begged, "Please – "

When she opened her eyes she thought the Earl was watching her, but he looked away so quickly that she could not be sure.

The carriage driver drove carefully, so as not to jolt the wounded man, yet Rona's nails ground into her palms at the slowness. Peter needed a warm bed and nursing.

"We're nearly there," said the Earl. "Don't worry, my dear. All will be well."

Madame Thierre was waiting for them at the house, all motherly concern. The doctor came in and got to work on Peter, replacing the hasty dressing that he had put on to staunch the blood with something more permanent. He administered some medicine which he said would help to prevent fever, and departed, promising to come again in the morning.

"I'll send a professional nurse," he said.

Madame Thierre was up in arms at the suggestion that she could not care for her guest herself.

"And I'm sure that Rona will be glad to help you," said the Earl quietly.

Rona turned quickly and laid her hand over his.

"I haven't thanked you yet for coming to save me."

"Never mind me," he said gruffly

"But you look so tired."

Then he said a strange thing. Patting her hand as a father might with a child, he told her,

"Never fear. All is well with me, I promise you."

They took the first turn together that night, sitting beside the bed, watching Peter's pale face, listening to his breathing that was mercifully steady.

"How did you come to be at that house?" Rona asked.

"We pursued your father and caught up with him," the Earl explained. "He told us that you had escaped and run to a man with a big moustache. It had to be Alexei, but he hadn't brought you home.

"That was when Peter told me everything. He's been working for British Intelligence all along."

"You hadn't known?"

"He told nobody. He let us all believe he was a devil-may-care young idler, always on the move because he cared for nothing but pleasure. The truth is that he's been on some dangerous assignments. He's been watching that pair for months, playing the gallant lover to the Countess as a way of keeping near her.

"He has had that house under surveillance all the time, and when it came to the point he was able to take us straight there."

"Emilia talked about 'the other half'," Rona recalled. "What did she mean by that?"

"The British and French governments have been working on a joint project. Do you know what a hydraulic pump is?"

"No."

"Neither do I. But according to Peter this one is revolutionary. Ten times as powerful as anything else of its kind, but very light. It might even have a military use.

"Apparently the inventors have this mad idea that one day it could be used to keep naval vessels beneath the water. Pure fantasy of course, but the two governments have been working on it and have just about finished the plans for the prototype.

"Every spy in Europe has been desperate to get their hands on those blueprints, but the Russians were ahead of the rest. They realised that each country only kept one half, and neither would make any sense until they were put together.

"In England they managed to get what they were after. Then it became a race to stop them getting the French half. That's what Peter has been doing here, keeping them under close watch."

He became silent as there was a movement from the bed. Slowly Peter opened his eyes and his gaze fell directly onto Rona. He did not speak, but no words were necessary.

In that moment everything was said in silence between them.

At last he reached out his hand and took hers.

"You are safe?" he asked in a croaking voice.

"Yes," she whispered. "I am safe."

He closed his eyes again.

The Earl crept quietly out of the room.

Rona stayed with Peter for another hour, until Madame Thierre came to relieve her. The colour was returning to his cheeks and she could leave him with an easier mind.

Outside she found the Earl waiting for her.

"A brief word with you," he said.

She knew she must have revealed her feelings for Peter and there was no use pretending now. But the Earl's calm face gave no sign of pain or upset. She could only guess how badly hurt he must be.

Now she braced herself for recriminations as they went down to the library.

But all he said was,

"My dear, I am to blame for not having seen the truth before. I was blind, believing what I wanted to believe. But of course, it was always Peter."

"Forgive me," she said, almost in tears at his melancholy kindness.

"There is nothing to forgive. I forced a situation on you when your father came. I made a joke then about taking advantage of you, but I didn't realise how literally true it was.

"Peter couldn't claim you because it would expose his courtship of the Countess as a fraud, which he dared not do. His duty to his country kept him silent, and I stepped in, not realising what damage I was doing. But you should have told me afterwards."

"How could we do anything to hurt you?" she asked. "We both care for you so much."

"Ah," he said quickly, as though she had thrust a dagger into him. "None of that. No sacrifices, please. That would be so undignified for all of us. Let us close the matter now."

He took her left hand and gazed for a moment at the diamond he had put there only a few hours ago. He slipped it off.

"There," he said cheerfully. "Now you are free."

But instead of releasing her hand at once, he lifted it up and laid his cheek against it.

"God bless you," he said.

"Giles – " It was the first time she had used his name. "You're so good to us. I hope that one day you'll find – "

"That's enough," he said with soft violence. "That's enough."

He dropped her hand and walked out of the room.

*

Through his contacts in high places Monsieur Thierre was able to fill in the rest of the story.

"They didn't take the real plans in London," he told Rona and the Earl. "They made copies and left the originals, so that it was a while before anyone knew they'd been tampered with. But luckily a message was sent here in time for us to get to work. When they got access to our side of the papers, the details had been changed. Even if the Rostoys had escaped to Russia, the plans would have been useless.

"But thanks to you and Peter they did not escape, and are now safely locked up in gaol. No harm has been done, except to poor Peter's shoulder, and the doctor says he should make a complete recovery."

*

Hour by hour Peter's strength returned. Sitting by his bed, watching him, Rona knew that this was her supreme happiness, and always would be.

"I love you with my all heart and my soul," he told her. "I've never loved anyone else."

"That's not what Alice says," Rona told him with a smile. "She talks a lot about your 'ladies'."

"My work has sometimes demanded a lot of flirting," he replied. "You saw that with the Countess. But true love is different. It's something I thought I would never find."

He took her hand in his.

"My heart was yours that first night at the ball, but I had to stay in the shadows. I wasn't even supposed to be in London. One of the guests that night was a dangerous man."

"Alexei?"

"No, one of his confederates. I had to watch and see who he talked to. But it was very hard to keep my mind on my work once I had met you.

"Even with your mask on, I knew you were the loveliest girl there. My heart was yours forever. But what could I do? My duty had to come first. All I could do was kiss you in a way I hoped you would never forget."

As he said these words he gave her a slight quizzical look.

Rona smiled.

"You were right. One kiss and I was yours. There was no hope for me. But I feared we would never meet again."

"So did I. I was afraid they would force you into that marriage, and it filled me with despair, because I knew you should marry only me. But I didn't see how it could ever happen. And then, when we met here I couldn't believe it."

"You didn't know me at first," she teased.

"Only because you made a guy of yourself in dowdy clothes and glasses. And I never saw your hair at the ball. But then I began to sense something about you.

"It was nothing to do with how you looked. It was more that I couldn't be near you without knowing the truth in all my senses. I think I knew finally when I held your hand in mine, on the boat. It was the hand I'd held that night."

"It was terrible to be near you, loving and wanting you, but unable to say so. And then to have to pretend to be in love with that woman, and watch you flirting with the

Count, all the time acting as though I didn't mind.

"That day in the park I wanted to be the one to save you and, but for mischance, I would have done. Instead I had to watch you carried away in his arms, and I think the sight sent me a little mad. When I came to see you next day I was wild and crazy with jealousy."

"Was that why you were so unpleasant?" Rona asked.

He groaned.

"I was, wasn't I? I didn't want to hurt you, but I was trying to keep you apart from him, partly for myself, and partly because by then I'd started to realise how dangerous he was.

"And all I could think of was to tell you it was improper for you to associate with him. I heard myself behaving abominably, but the right words wouldn't come. And then you collapsed, and I hated myself."

And now Peter added,

"But I hope that you will forgive me."

"I would forgive you anything," she replied simply.

He took her hand in his, and smiled, looking at it.

"To think this little hand pulled me through that window," he said. "Where did you get the strength?"

"From my love," she said at once. "Nothing is stronger than that."

"Yes," he said, nodding. "Nothing is stronger than love, or I would have fallen. Since I met you again my love has grown stronger every day, but I had to hide it and pretend to be that woman's slave.

"I know my behaviour puzzled you, the times I was absent without explanation, the times I barely noticed you because I was pretending to be at her feet. I could only pray that you would understand when finally I could explain."

"There's only one thing I really want to know," said

Rona. "Were you the man in the dressing room at Ginette's, the man who bought Emilia that red dress."

"Yes. But I promise you that the bill went straight back to London, to be paid by my employers."

She smiled.

"That's all right then."

He looked at her anxiously. "You will marry me, won't you? I neglected to ask you."

"Don't be silly," she laughed. "Of course I'll marry you. But my darling, I'm afraid I won't have a dowry to bring you. My father will be so angry that he'll cut me off without a penny."

"Good. Then you'll know I'm not a fortune hunter."

"I've been thinking about how we should live after the wedding – yes, I even thought of that before you asked me. Wasn't that scandalous of me?"

"Shameless!" he said, smiling tenderly at her.

"I think I should join you in the Secret Service. I obviously have a talent for it, and two of us working together – "

"Would be spotted at once," he interrupted hastily. "I'm leaving the Service. The Rostoys weren't working alone, and I should think I'm too well known by now to be any further use. You as well."

"That's a pity. Before you were shot I was beginning to enjoy it. It was thrilling to talk to Emilia and trick her into revealing things because she thought I already knew. I told her I'd guessed all along that Alexei was her husband, and she hadn't really been very clever. You should have seen her face!"

"I wish I had," he said appreciatively. "It's a shame that you can't be a spy, my darling, because you obviously have a talent for it. Not to mention your unsuspected athletic prowess in pulling me through that window."

He sighed wistfully.

"What a team we would have made. But that's in the past. Mr. and Mrs. Carlton are going to live a sedate life."

"Lovely. In a cottage, with chickens. I've always wanted to do that."

"We'll do no such thing. We'll live in a little manor that I own in the country. It's not as grand as Giles' house, but I think we might well be very happy in it."

"If we're together I'll be happy," she said at once.

"There's another reason I want to leave the Service," he said. "I was growing weary of it. My whole life was lived among lies, deceit, betrayal, being one thing, pretending to be another, never able to be truly honest."

"That's what I sensed in you that first night," Rona remembered. "We were speaking of the betrayal of trust, and suddenly I had the feeling that you were being crushed by a great burden."

"Yes, I knew you sensed something. Our minds were so much in harmony even then. And that harmony will keep us close, always."

"We're going to be so happy."

"Yes." He turned her left hand over in his, noticing the bare place where the ring had been. "But there will always be one cloud. I can't stop feeling bad about Giles."

"I don't think he would like you to do that," she said seriously. "He would consider it undignified."

"Why do you say that?"

"It was something he said when he told me that I was 'free'. Giles is a proud man. He doesn't want our pity, and would be offended by it."

"Yes," he sighed. "I know you're right. Oh my darling, I love you, I love you so much."

She could not answer. Her eyes were wet with tears.

"And tomorrow," he continued, "I will love you even more than I do today. As the years pass we'll know the true depth of our love. Just as I was meant for you, you were meant for me."

Very gently he put his hand under her chin and turned her face to his.

"Tell me that you love me," he whispered.

"I didn't know it was possible to love anyone as I love you," she said.

Then Peter's lips found hers. She knew that he was giving her his heart, just as she gave hers to him.

And so it would be, always.

*

As soon as Peter was well, they were married. It was arranged quickly for fear of any further raids by her father.

The night before the wedding the Earl spoke quietly to his daughter.

"I know that Miss Johnson has taught you some important lessons about love," he said. "Well, now you father has one for you, and it is this. You cannot order somebody to love you. What a simple world it would be if we could!"

He sighed.

"But it can't be done. If the one you love cannot give you his heart fully and freely, then you must let him go, without resentment or self pity."

But Alice was very young, and not easy to convince. "How could they do it to you, Papa?"

"My child," he said very seriously, "nobody has done me any wrong. We were all the victims of circumstances. Peter and Rona are still our family and we must keep them close. How foolish it would be to behave in such a way that there was a split in the family. Then we would lose both of them. That must not be allowed to happen. That's why we will both play our parts at the wedding tomorrow."

"But how can you bear it?" Alice asked with tears in her eyes.

"Because I still have you," he said, holding her tightly. "And in time the sadness will pass."

*

The wedding was simple. The Thierre family joined them in the English Church in Peter's village. Monsieur Thierre gave the bride away, the Earl was Peter's groomsman, and Alice was the chief bridesmaid with Agnes and Cecile following.

Later that night, when they were alone together and the house was quiet and still, they stood locked in each other's arms for a long time, free at last to enjoy their love.

"I want to show you something," Rona said at last.

Reaching under her pillow she took out the little porcelain Harlequin that he had given her.

"I was going to ask you what he meant," she said, "but I didn't get the chance."

"But you knew what he meant," said Peter, smiling at her tenderly.

"Yes. I've cherished him, keeping him under my pillow. Now I don't need to hide him. No more masks, no more secrets, ever again in our lives."

She turned out the lamp and her husband took her into his arms again, holding her close so that her heart beat against his.

The room was dark except for the moonlight shining through the windows. It fell on the Harlequin figurine, giving him a strange look.

Almost like a smile of contentment.